AGAINST A
RISING TIDE

SAMANTHA CAYTO

Against a Rising Tide
ISBN # 978-1-83943-730-4
©Copyright Samantha Cayto 2021
Cover Art by Louisa Maggio ©Copyright June 2021
Interior text design by Claire Siemaszkiewicz
Pride Publishing

AGAINST A
RISING TIDE

Dedication

I dedicate this book to DD—she knows who she is—for her constant friendship, support and generous help. She was the first person to welcome me into the sisterhood of romance writers. I don't know where I'd be without her.

Chapter One

By the time Scott reached the beach house, visions of falling face-down in his bed swam before his eyes. He really should have checked into one of the airport hotels for the night instead of renting a car and heading north. But the driving need for solitude had overridden his better judgment. Even arriving in Boston at o-dark-thirty hadn't thinned the crowds of people enough to satisfy his jangled nerves. He needed quiet and the mental space that came from being utterly alone to get his head screwed back on right. Otherwise, his time in the SEAL Teams would come to an end. The mere thought of having to leave his Naval career was intolerable to him.

He took a moment as he exited his rental SUV to simply stand and stare out over the ocean. The sun was just rising above the rippling blue-green water, washing the horizon in tones of red and orange. Seagulls screeched in their staccato fashion, as if they were in a constant state of agitation. He welcomed the familiar sound of their mindless scolding. The crash of waves against the rocky shore told him the tide was coming in. He took in a deep breath of salty air tinged with a hint of clam flats and smiled. All the joy of his childhood filled the aching hole that had formed in the middle of his chest. Coming here had been the right call. This was where he needed to be.

His exhaustion momentarily abated, Scott grabbed his duffel bag from the back of the SUV and walked up the stone path to the front door. There was no need to lock his vehicle, not in the low-crime town of Sewall, Massachusetts. It was barely more than a spit of rocky land and had never developed the cachet of its neighbors like Rockport as a fashionable seaside town. It attracted no one other than the dedicated perennial vacationer and was the perfect place to hide away for a while without fear of disturbance. His sister wouldn't haul her brood up from the suburbs of Boston until August. He could be sure of having the place all to himself...to be alone.

Safe.

No, where had that thought come from? He was a SEAL, for God's sake. There was nowhere on Earth that he didn't feel as if he could protect himself. And he understood better than most that death was always lurking around, regardless. One only had to be ready to face it. Defeat it. If necessary, accept it when options had truly run out, but only after fighting to the very last breath. He took in another deep lungful of brisk ocean air with that last thought, irritated at his dark, almost defeatist attitude.

I need sleep. That's all.

Scott almost sprinted to the seafoam green door, fumbled with the keys to open it and stepped inside the cool, quiet house of his childhood…that was *not* empty.

He froze inside the doorway and stared at the vision that greeted him. His mind did all kinds of acrobatics as he tried to make sense of what he saw. With the open floorplan of the first floor, he had a clear view of a naked woman standing in the kitchen. She was reaching up to a shelf filled with bowls, her toned arm stretched high. A curtain of long, dark hair swung below her shoulder blades, catching his attention. He followed the movement past the tapered ends, down a slender back of creamy skin accentuated by some kind of colorful tramp-stamp.

The tattoo skimmed a high, tight ass that held his gaze like a magnet. His overtired brain popped and snapped with a sudden spark of need. As exhausted as he was, his body came alive, desire shooting through him to pool in his groin. Even as an involuntary grunt passed his lips, the more rational part of his mind took over. It was trying to put on the brakes because something was off. The woman's hips were too straight, and her shoulders were a bit broad. As the pieces clicked into place, the beach house inhabitant whirled around with a sharp inhalation. Now, the cock and balls of the *man* came literally swinging into view.

Scott's own cock was caught between hardening and deflating again. He could feel it waging a war inside his worn jeans for a few seconds before it gave up in a semi-hard state that he ignored. *Nothing to see here, folks.* It was the other man's reaction that caught and held his focus. Across the large expanse, there was visible fear in the dark eyes staring back at him. And the guy did nothing to hide his genitals. Instead, one hand had flown to the base of his throat in a clear defensive gesture. He whipped the other up to hold against his left cheek. But the quickness of the move hadn't stopped Scott from seeing a livid bruise that marred the pretty skin there.

"Who?" The young man blinked at him for a few seconds, breathing quickly, before he visibly relaxed. "Oh, you're Karen's brother, aren't you?" Although he dropped the one hand from his throat, he didn't let go of his cheek entirely. Instead, he carded his fingers through his hair, letting the strands hide that half of his face. "She said you were overseas."

"I was." Scott stepped fully into the house and shut the door behind him before setting his duffel on the floor. He was careful to keep his movements slow. He'd dealt with petrified villagers plenty of times and knew he had to prove that he wasn't a danger to them. *Build trust.* While he was at a loss as to why exactly, he could sense this man needed the same kind of consideration.

"I just got back and have two weeks' leave." Not that it had been his idea.

"Take the time, Carpenter. There's no shame in needing it after what you've been through."

"Yes, sir."

He'd known an order when he'd been given one, but he still felt some guilt about lying around on a beach while others were out there fighting on his behalf. He pushed those thoughts aside to deal with the more pressing matter. Before he could ask the who, what and why, the naked man was talking again.

"I guess Karen didn't know that. She said I could stay here until she comes up with her kids." He dropped his gaze, while still tugging at his hair in nervous fashion.

Scott approached the kitchen area, again keeping his movements slow and non-threatening. "I was going to call her later." He stopped and hooked his thumbs in his front pockets. "I'm sorry. You have me at a disadvantage. Do I know you?"

The young man flashed his gaze at him before skittering it away. Now that he was closer, Scott could see that his eyes weren't entirely brown. There was a hint of green there as well. Hazel, he supposed, although he'd never given much thought to eye color before. He forced himself to focus on them, however, because the alternative was to stare farther south. There was a temptation to sneak peeks at parts of the man's body. He'd always studiously avoided that urge before. He saw more naked men than he did women, that was for sure, and in a military environment where privacy was non-existent, one had to be respectful. Inside a quaint New England house, with the muted dawn shining through the window, making everything soft and almost romantic, the nudity was harder to ignore.

"I'm Kitt Tyler."

Scott's attention was tugged back to Kitt's face—although really, to his lips. He couldn't help noticing how plump and pink they were. 'Generous' was the word that came to mind, like those of old-time movie starlets—the type of mouth that combat men dreamed of kissing as they lay in their makeshift beds. It was what got them up again, fighting for their country. That observation startled him even more. *What the hell is my problem?* Exhaustion, that was all. What he needed was a solid eight horizontal hours uninterrupted, and that wasn't going to happen until he wrapped up this unexpected meet-and-greet.

"You're a friend of Karen's?" *Kind of a dumb question.*

Kitt gnawed briefly at his lower lip, once again drawing Scott's unwilling attention to that spot. "Yeah, I am, but also her hairdresser. I mean, that's how we first met, and we've become friends, too. You know?"

No, Scott didn't...at all. The last thing he and his sister ever talked about was hair styling, although she always looked great. He knew that she prided herself on being elegant and fashionable for her job as a publisher for some glossy, high-end magazine. She had him on her subscription list, which was sweet, except it all went straight into his trash. What did he care about trendy places to eat in Boston and the best store for thousand-thread-count sheets?

"Anyway," the guy continued, still playing with his hair and darting his gaze around. "She has like a million pictures of you at home, so I recognized you straight off."

Not exactly true. For a moment, when he'd turned and caught sight of Scott, Kitt had obviously been afraid. *Of what?* Scott wondered. *Or rather...whom?*

Scott ran a hand over his head. The need for sleep was overtaking his initial and visceral reaction to this unexpected guest. "I'm sure she's bored you to tears with stories about me, too." His sister was proud of his service, although he feared that she'd put him on a pedestal he didn't deserve, certainly not after this last deployment.

A ghost of a smile graced Kitt's lips. That was the moment when it hit Scott that this young man was utterly gorgeous—at a he-could-be-a-model level. Although, he was probably too short for that profession. He was about five-seven, just the right height to tuck into Scott's shoulder. The new observations sent his brain into another unwanted spasm of discord.

"She has a bit, but I think it's great how close you two are." Releasing his hold on his hair, Kitt fluttered his hands and shifted his feet. "Anyway, I'll pack up and get out of your way. It, um, might take a while for me to get a Lyft driver to come here this early, though. I hope that's okay."

"You don't have a car?" Another stupid question. The driveway had been empty when he'd pulled up.

"No. Um, no." Kitt stared at the floor again.

Scott could see the distress in the guy's posture and read it in his expression. He knew when someone was afraid, nervous or angry, even when they tried to hide it from him. He could tell when they were lying about something. Kitt Tyler wasn't merely a friend of his sister who needed a free summer vacation. There was more to it than that, and given the guy's skittishness and that bruise on his cheek, Scott could make an educated guess what that *more* was.

For the moment, however, he was incapable of any further rational thought. He needed that eight hours, then he'd deal with the situation.

"Look," he said, repressing a yawn. "I've been awake for over forty-eight hours straight. I'm going upstairs to get some sleep. No need for you to leave yet. We'll talk later."

Kitt's relief was easy to see. Still, he said, "Are you sure?"

"Absolutely." Scott turned to retrieve his duffel bag from by the door.

"Oh, I should get dressed now so that I don't disturb you."

Too late on that score. "I can sleep through anything, but thanks."

He made himself not watch as Kitt flitted up the stairs. He didn't rush when he followed, either, so that he wouldn't see any more of that undeniably tantalizing flesh. His plan worked. By the time he'd reached the second floor, his sister's guest had disappeared into the far back room. The sounds of a drawer opening and closing drifted down the narrow hallway. Scott bit back a groan when he realized that Kitt had taken his usual room. That thought had barely formed before the guy popped back out, wearing crotch-hugging cut-off jeans and a tight white crop top. The clothing wasn't much better than the nudity had been at hiding the guy's fit physique. Oh, and bonus, now that Scott wasn't studiously averting his gaze, he could see a belly button ring winking from the flat stomach.

"I took one of the kid's rooms, if that's okay?" Kitt looked impossibly young himself. What was the minimum age to be a hairdresser, eighteen? The guy must be straight out of school.

Scott didn't bother to correct him. Visions of Kitt lying in Scott's bed were already creeping into his brain. Instead, he waved the issue away and turned into what had been his parents' old room. Karen and her husband used it now, but she obviously wasn't coming up any time soon. He may as well bed down in it. He kicked the door shut with more force than he'd intended, but the lure of the big brass bed was irresistible. Stumbling toward it, he did as he'd dreamed of for hours—fell face-down onto the quilt his grandmother had made. He had just enough brainpower left to kick off his sneakers before giving in to the pull of sleep.

His last thought, however, was of the pretty boy at the end of the hall, silhouetted by the glint of the rising sun.

* * * *

Kitt gnawed at the side of his thumb while he watched the clock on his new phone advance minute-by-minute until it was eight o'clock. He knew he was being overly anxious, but he couldn't do anything else. It had taken tremendous willpower not to call Karen the moment her brother had shut himself in the master bedroom. After a pathetic attempt to stuff some food into his jittery stomach, he'd settled in the living room, watching the tide come in and begging time to advance quicker.

He'd managed to amuse himself for a few minutes with the apps on the phone Karen had bought him. It was a significant upgrade from his old one, with a new number, a necessary step to keep Emilio from harassing him with calls and texts. Besides, Kitt was certain his ex had inserted a tracking app on the old one. With that thing lying in a Boston dump, there was no way to find him. The thought of being discovered sent a shiver through him. He was incredibly grateful for his good luck in having Karen as a friend as well as a client. She was a generous woman who knew how to get things done. She'd had Kitt out of the city and safely installed in her Sewall house within hours of his arriving, crying, at her doorstep. Someday he would repay her, although the how and when were too hard for him to think about at the moment.

Hunching his shoulders, he switched his gaze to the beautiful view of the ocean, then back to the digital screen on his phone. His lovely surroundings were lost on him. His anxiety was overwhelming, especially when he tried to figure out what he'd do next. Without money or family, his options were almost non-existent. Tears threatened to spill over his cheeks. He swiped at his eyes impatiently. Crying was not going to solve anything.

The moment when he saw that it was time for Karen to be out of her house and on her way to work, he called. He hated being dependent on anyone, but at least Karen didn't make him feel guilty. She seemed genuinely happy to help. Her number was the only one stored so far on the new phone, and he intended it to stay that way in the foreseeable future. He didn't trust anyone else he knew to keep his secret safe from Emilio. When he'd needed to count on them the most, he'd realized that all his so-called friends were either more loyal to his ex than to him or too shallow to care about his plight.

"All men are the same, honey. Just give him a BJ, and he'll calm down."

Karen picked up on the second ring, her voice echoing through the Bluetooth of her car. "What's wrong?"

"Nothing," he was quick to assure her. "I didn't mean to scare you."

Her breath whooshed over the line. "Thank God, you nearly gave me a heart attack. It's only been a day and a half. Is there something you need?"

Kitt thought of the mountain of groceries that Karen had bought him at the small convenience store in town, along with books and magazines, in case there was nothing interesting on the bazillion cable channels she had at the house. Because he couldn't use his credit cards or access his bank account without giving his location away, he'd been dependent on her to buy his necessities. The consummate host, she'd made sure he was well provisioned before leaving.

"Nothing, sweetie, you've thought of everything… except your brother arrived a couple of hours ago."

"Scott?" She practically squealed in a very un-Karen-like way. "He's back in the country? Why didn't the dope call me?"

"Um…" Kitt wasn't sure how to respond to that. It wasn't as if the man had been particularly forthcoming, and it was possible he'd said more than Kitt remembered. It had been hard to concentrate on anything other than the initial shock of fear, followed by the overwhelming draw of the large, hyper-masculine presence. "He was exhausted, I think. Needed to sleep first."

Kitt pictured Karen's brother's hollowed-out look. The man's eyes had told a deeper story than mere tiredness. There had been a haunted expression in them. He knew it well, given how often he'd seen it in the mirror.

"He still should have called me." There was a blare of a horn and Karen let out a ripe, Boston-based swear before speaking again. "How long is he planning on staying up there?"

"I think he said something about a two-week leave." Kitt bit his lower lip and frowned. His gaze wandered up to the ceiling and a vision of that tall, broad man lying in bed popped into his head. He couldn't help but wonder if the guy had taken the time to strip first, what position he slept in, was he on top of the covers or lying under a sheet? Not that any of that was his concern, but he couldn't stop the thoughts or keep from wincing when it all reminded him of how they'd first met.

"I was in the kitchen buck-naked when he arrived. It was so embarrassing when I realized it, but I didn't want to draw attention to the fact that my dick was swinging right in front of his eyes. I kind of pretended I didn't care."

His cheeks warmed at the memory. Then the aforementioned dick pulsed as if it had a different view of what had happened. *Weird.* His libido had been in hiding for quite some time. He touched the painful bruise on the side of his face, a constant reminder at the moment of why that was so.

Karen laughed. "I can assure you Scott thought nothing of it. He's a SEAL, remember? He and his teammates live in each other's pockets for months at a time. Seeing another man naked is an everyday event for him, I bet. Be forewarned that he sometimes forgets to shut the bathroom door, he's so used to letting it all hang out."

Kitt eyes popped at the idea that the sailor might be the next one to wander around the beach house nude. His cheeks got even hotter. The reality of his situation set in a second later. "I won't be around to worry about it. I've got to pack and get out of here. Is it okay if I use the Lyft app you downloaded for me?"

God, he hated the idea of spending more of Karen's money. Plus, he had no idea where he was going to go.

"That's what it's there for, silly. But you don't have to leave. Scott didn't try to kick you out, did he?"

"No, not at all," he hurried to assure her. He didn't want to be the cause of any conflict between the siblings. "He told me to stick around until he woke up, anyway."

Kitt stood and wandered over to the big bay window overlooking the rocky shore. The small beach area below the house was almost completely covered with water. "But we both know I have to go, and there's no point in waiting. We thought I'd have this place to myself. With your brother here, I can't stay. He'll want privacy."

Besides, how could Kitt stand being cooped up with the guy? The vacation home had been adorably quaint and cozy while he'd been on his own. With the man's sudden entrance, it had shrunk to almost dollhouse proportions. He didn't think his nerves could take the proximity of someone whose masculine heat and scent had crossed an entire room to assault Kitt's every sense. It would be a constant effort to avoid the unavoidable. He was *so* done tiptoeing around a desirable man who also had the potential to be volatile and dangerous.

Karen was talking again, forcing him out of his own head. "…not his call. Our parents left that house to both of us. We have an equal right to use it. If he wanted it now, he should have said so. If he intends to spend his leave up there, he'll just have to share it with you."

"Karen…" he started to argue.

"Kitt, it's fine. You need somewhere to lie low while my lawyer friend does her job to keep you safe legally. Please, stay there for me, if not for yourself. I'm worried about you."

Kitt had to smile at that. She really was the only person he could count on. "Oh, sweetie, I promise I won't do anything stupid, like leave without telling you. I don't want to cause you any trouble. *More* trouble, that is." Because Karen had already put herself out by helping him.

"This is what friends do for each other. Stop acting as if you're a burden." There was a screeching of brakes and more cursing. "Now, leave Scott to me. He's pretty easygoing and will probably split his time between sitting around watching baseball and running suicide drills on the beach. Plus, he'll likely hit the bars in the evening to pick up women. He has no qualms about doing *that*. Half the time, he'll spend the night somewhere else." Kitt pictured her eyes rolling. "He won't disturb you at all."

That was not what Kitt was worried about. *He* was the interloper, not Scott. And he could easily imagine that the guy never had any problems hooking up. What woman would resist six-foot-three, two-hundred-and-God-knew-how-many-pounds worth of jacked Navy SEAL?

I certainly can't. Nope, not going there. Bad idea. Stupendously bad. I've sworn off men and the guy is not even gay.

It wasn't hard to give in to Karen, either. Kitt didn't want to leave. "Okay, I'll let you handle it, but promise me if he doesn't want me here, you'll tell me."

Karen snorted. "If you insist. It's not going to be an issue, though." There was a pregnant pause. "You're not afraid of him, are you?"

"No." It was almost not a lie. On a knee-jerk level, the man did scare him. What bothered him more was the primitive attraction that he felt for Scott. He didn't want that. He was so done with wanting unsuitable men.

"Good, because unless you're a terrorist, he would never hurt you. In fact, now that I think about it, it's a good thing he's there. He'll be great protection."

"No!" The word had popped out louder than he'd intended. Kitt held his breath and glanced at the ceiling, listening for any indication that he'd woken his unexpected housemate. There was nothing except the constant sound of the waves crashing and the gulls screeching as they circled above the house.

He let out his breath. "Sorry. I meant, please don't tell him why I'm here. It's, um, embarrassing."

Kitt hated the fact that he'd gotten himself into this situation. When it came to men, he had consistently made the worst choices, forming relationships even after seeing the warning signs. No matter what Karen or the lawyer had told him, he couldn't shake the belief that this was all his fault.

"Okay, if that's what you want. You've done nothing wrong, you know?" When Kitt didn't respond, she blew noisily into the phone. "Relax. Please. I'll handle Scott."

"Don't call him yet," Kitt said hurriedly. "He's asleep and probably will be for hours." Which was kind of a dumb thing to remind her of. She knew that. Except he felt oddly protective of the guy. He needed his sleep.

"Yup, I get it. I'll wait to call him until after work. If I haven't spoken to him by the time you next see him, have him call me."

"Okay."

"Have a relaxing day. And, Kitt?"

"Yeah?"

"Everything's going to be all right."

"Sure." He put as much optimism as he could in his reply, but deep down he didn't believe it. He couldn't quite imagine that anything would be right ever again.

Chapter Two

Scott woke exactly eight hours after falling asleep. It was a weird and useful quirk of his brain that he could set an internal alarm clock to wake him after however many hours or minutes he wanted. He was back to being his usual alert self, although not exactly feeling fresh, given that he'd failed to open any windows or turn on the air conditioning unit. The room was stuffy, and as a result, he felt both sticky and dehydrated. Neither of those things bothered him, being merely passing observations as he shoved to a sitting position. He was grateful to be alone when he saw that he'd drooled all over his sister's sham pillow. She would not appreciate that, given the meticulous way she'd decorated the old house in the years since they'd inherited the place.

Naturally, that led to thoughts of why he'd bedded down in her room and not his own. Being an experienced special operator, he didn't need much time to remind himself of his sitrep. He knew where he was and, more importantly, with whom. He grimaced as he mulled the information with a clearer head. His hoped-for sanctuary was nothing of the kind. Instead, it had turned out to be a beach house game of musical rooms not of his making.

Scott stretched, yawned and scratched his belly while planning his next move. It was always best to tackle the biggest issues first. That meant ignoring his full bladder and his empty stomach and addressing the immediate problem that Kitt Tyler presented. Pulling his phone out of his pocket, he called his sister.

"I was going to try you when I left work." Typical Karen, she wasted no time.

"Hello to you too, sis." Scott didn't let her abruptness bother him. Their relationship was solid...always had been.

"People who don't bother to let their loved ones know when they have returned safe and sound from God knows where do not deserve the usual courtesies."

He winced at her frosty rebuke. It was no more than he deserved. "Sorry. You're right. I just...got on the plane to Boston before I even knew for sure what my plan was." So lame, but he wasn't ready to admit how much he was struggling at the moment. Everything was still too raw.

Karen knew him well enough that he needn't have worried on that account. Her tone softened with her next breath. "I understand. I'm being pissy because I didn't expect Kitt's staying there would be a problem."

"Right—and that's why I'm calling." As he spoke, he stood and wandered over to the windows that overlooked the beach. The tide was already on its way out again, but the view of the wide expanse of ocean once more helped to ease that ache in his chest. "I assume he called and gave you the full story."

Karen chuckled, confirming no detail had been left out. "He did. I assured him that you don't shock easily."

Shocked? No, he hadn't been. Disturbed? That was something altogether different, not that he'd admit it to his sister. "I *was* surprised to walk in and find him here, but as you've more or less pointed out, that was on me. I should have told you I was flying back east."

He peered straight down at the large boulders lining the shore. A flash of white caught his attention. Kitt was bounding around the rocks wearing the same top and cut-offs that he'd put on earlier. Only now, his hair was pulled back into a ponytail that bounced with each leap. Scott's breath caught at a particularly dramatic hop from one rock to another. He almost threw open the window and called down to the boy to go back to the sandy spit of land. It was dangerous to romp along the shore. Except that would have been ridiculous. Hadn't he and his sister done the same thing long ago in their childhood? Kitt wasn't a little boy, either. He was a grown man…sort of.

"How old is he, anyway, fifteen?" he heard himself ask before his intelligence could catch up to his tongue. He mentally facepalmed.

There was a telling pause before Karen answered. "Twenty-two, as it happens."

"Still a baby," he muttered, again before he could self-censor. Maybe he should have waited to call his sister after all. He wasn't as alert as he'd thought.

"Says the old man who is barely past thirty."

By SEAL standards, that was an advanced age. Spec ops was a young man's game. It wouldn't be much longer before he found himself benched. His back and knees were already making themselves known with not-so-subtle twinges each day. And it wasn't only the physical problems that were warning him that his time in the Teams was almost up. The mental toll was mounting as well, especially after this last mission. So yeah, he felt every one of his thirty years—a weight bearing him down. He didn't say any of that to his sister, however. She had enough on her plate without him adding his crap to it.

Scott turned away from the window and the sight of his pretty houseguest frolicking. "Sorry... I'm off point. What are we going to do about him?"

"Nothing. I told Kitt he could stay. He has nowhere else to go at the moment."

Scott grimaced again and rubbed the back of his neck. This wasn't surprising news. "I assume that his own home is out of the question, given that someone has been beating on him." The memory of the bruise stark against the boy's pale skin caused his blood pressure to spike, nearly taking his head off. Nothing ticked him off more than what he had to assume was a man using his brute strength against someone weaker and apparently in need of protection.

Karen huffed. "I promised him I wouldn't discuss any of that, but you're a smart boy, Scott, particularly good at adding two and two."

"Yeah, yeah." He paced over to the bed and sat heavily. "I'm not trying to be an asshole, Kar. I was hoping for some peace and quiet for a few days. I suppose I could go to a motel."

"No! That would be silly. We used to jam eight of us in that house when Grammy was alive, and the twins were babies. The two of you will have plenty of room to carve out for yourselves."

Scott had to smile at the mention of happier days. For a couple of very special years, they'd had the benefit of four generations sharing magical times together. Things had changed very quickly, and now, other than more distant relatives, all the family Scott had was his sister, her husband and their two children. He knew they'd do anything for him, and likewise he would literally die for them. Griping about Kitt's presence — something obviously important to Karen — was cowardly. And really, if he couldn't handle one other person being in a house with him, he was washed up as an operator.

"You're right, of course. It's not like I have to entertain him."

"You certainly don't, and if you're lucky, he'll cook for you. He's wonderful, really. If he weren't such a fabulous hair cutter and colorist, I'd encourage him to become a professional chef."

"I don't expect him to play homemaker for me." As he said the words, however, the idea of Kitt buzzing around the kitchen on his behalf had more appeal than he was comfortable with. "I only want some solitude. That's all. He's, ah, hard to ignore."

"Oh, Scott Carpenter, you're not worried that some of Kitt's gay is going to rub off on you?"

Scott clenched his jaw briefly before he retorted, "No, Karen Carpenter, you know damn well I'm not." He deliberately used her maiden name when mad at her, knowing how much she hated it. There had been endless teasing for both of them in childhood over carrying famous people's names. Karen had been delighted with the opportunity to ditch the association with the late, great singer, while he'd always been amused when asked if he were related to the astronaut, especially once he'd joined the Navy.

"I am *not* homophobic. A member of the Teams recently came out and no one was overtly hostile about it." Although, he didn't add, private reactions hadn't been as kind or accepting. Being gay was not viewed so far as being 'career-boosting'. "*I* certainly couldn't have cared less. My position has been clear on this. Any guy willing to cover my ass is welcome to stare at it while doing so, too."

"I know." She sounded contrite, taking the sudden wind of indignation out of his sails. "I'm just saying that he'll be low-maintenance and he really needs a quiet place to hang out for a while. But I also know that he's someone who commands attention simply by being himself."

Man, Scott didn't need his sister to tell him how compelling Kitt was. That was Scott's problem, though. Kitt obviously had enough to worry about and didn't need Scott's fascination with him and the resulting discomfort to be added to the list. Scott had been in too many places in the world where women had to restrict their lives so that men didn't lose their shit, instead of the men controlling their own actions and reactions. He wasn't about to pull the same crap on Kitt.

"I'll deal," was all he said, because that was the right answer.

Someone's voice in his sister's background came through the connection. "Oops," she said, "got to go. I'm late for a meeting. Just be chill with Kitt and we'll talk again in a few days, okay?"

"Sure, sis."

She didn't hang up right away. "Scott, you're all right, aren't you?"

"I'm fine. What could possibly happen to me in Sewall?" He deliberately misinterpreted her question because he couldn't go there—not yet.

"That's not what I meant, but okay, be that way. Bye."

"Bye." The connection was already broken.

Scott tossed the phone on the bed and padded into the attached bathroom. Hungry as he was, he needed to first relieve himself, then freshen up. He could go for weeks on a mission with no washing of any kind without thinking twice about it. Once he was back in a place with indoor plumbing, he couldn't stand feeling grubby.

A quick shower cleared any lingering malaise. He threw on a clean pair of jeans and a T-shirt before heading downstairs. He approached the first floor as if he were clearing a building in a combat zone, cautiously checking that Kitt hadn't returned to the house. It was absolutely ridiculous, but he couldn't stop himself. The place was empty, and he breathed a small sigh of relief. Something to eat would set him right and chase away this strange unease he felt about his situation, regardless of what he'd told Karen.

The kitchen was spotless, although items drying in the rack on the counter told him that Kitt had cooked in some fashion while Scott had slept. He'd heard nothing, so the guy must have been careful not to make much noise. Opening the refrigerator, he saw a tall glass pitcher of iced tea with a Post-it note stuck to it that said 'drink me'. Beside it was a large plastic storage bowl that had its own note saying 'eat me'.

He ruthlessly suppressed the juvenile response to the words and pulled out both items. After pouring a big glass of iced tea, downing it in one long swallow, then pouring a second glass, he opened the food container. Inside was a cold pasta salad with chunks of chicken and avocados, cherry tomatoes, what appeared to be feta cheese and ripe olives. Saliva pooled in his mouth just looking at it. Man, he was suddenly not merely hungry but famished. He piled a plate high, then took his meal to the table by the bay window that overlooked the back deck. He settled in the way he had a thousand times before, with his bare feet resting on the edge of the window seat and tipping his chair back on two legs. As he shoveled the food into his mouth like a starving man, he took in the show that his houseguest was unwittingly giving.

Kitt had returned to the sandy part of the beach, although in this part of Massachusetts, he would always be walking on rocks. It was only a matter of the size. When the tide was out, there were softer spots to access. With the receding water, there was still just a pebble beach available. Kitt walked gingerly away from the house with his head down. Every once in a while, he'd stop to pick something up, examine it, then either stick it into the pocket of his shorts or toss it away. Scott couldn't help smiling. How many times had he and Karen done the same thing as kids? Even now, there remained a stash of beach treasure in a basket in his room — rather, Kitt's room at the moment. Had the guy seen it and been inspired to add to it?

Scott shook his head at the sentimental thoughts. He stood abruptly with his now-empty dish and drained his glass once more. Then he returned to the kitchen to rinse his plate and stick it in the dishwasher. He poured more iced tea, hesitating briefly at taking so much before deciding that he could make some himself later to replenish the pitcher. A sudden craving for something sweet sent him to the old-fashioned cookie jar that had belonged to his grammy. He didn't really expect to find anything there, so was surprised when it turned out to be filled with oatmeal raisin cookies — clearly homemade, not store-bought. Kitt had been very busy in the past eight hours. Scott devoured one while standing at the counter. It was delicious — soft and chewy, almost still warm.

Grabbing three more, Scott returned to the living room area, steering for the reclining chair in front of the TV at the last minute. Really, that made a lot more sense than staring out the back. There had to be a game on that would hold his interest more than watching a stranger play on the beach. *Plus, it's kind of creepy for me to turn my house guest into a form of entertainment, isn't it?* With effort, he turned on a sports channel and forced himself to become invested in watching the Red Sox probably lose another game and forget that yards away, a too-pretty young man was frolicking on the edge of the foamy sea.

* * * *

Being outdoors had done Kitt a world of good. There was something about the salty air and sunshine that had lifted his spirits. Plus, he'd worked off nervous energy running across the rocks that no amount of cooking or cleaning had accomplished. He wouldn't have dared leave the house even a day ago because he was so worried about Emilio scooping him up and dragging him back to their apartment in Boston. It didn't matter how much Karen reassured him that there was no way for him to be found. Having lived with his boyfriend's obsessive control for so long had made him feel that the man was invincible. Somehow, though, knowing that Karen's brother was there had given him the courage to venture outside.

It was strange. The big man's presence should have made him more anxious, not less. And it had, at first. But as the morning had worn on, he'd become used to the idea of sharing the space with him. It was only a matter of being useful without being intrusive. To that end, he'd cooked and baked, knowing that once Scott woke, he'd be looking for a good meal. Kitt tried not to think of it as bribing the man or falling back on the habits of trying to appease male anger. He thought of it, instead, as showing comforting domesticity. Besides, it was a way to repay his friend for her kindness. She'd appreciate his looking after her brother.

And what Kitt got out of it was the sudden realization that going outdoors would be safe so long as he stuck close to the house. If anything happened, he could call for Scott to come to his rescue. He wasn't sure why he was convinced that was the case. He simply knew. Perhaps it was because Karen had always spoken of her brother in heroic terms. He was the kind of man who rushed toward danger while others ran from it. Karen had absolute faith in her brother, so Kitt felt he could, as well.

With the afternoon waning, he figured it was okay to return to the house. Scott was probably up by now, and if not, Kitt could remain quiet. He rinsed the sand off his feet under the faucet installed at the bottom of the outside stairs before heading to the top of the deck. He could see Scott sitting inside with his back to him, watching a baseball game. God, he hoped the Sox won. Men could get so angry when their team lost. He almost turned and went back to the beach, except that would be ridiculous. He either trusted that it was safe to be in the house with Scott, or he'd have to leave after all. It was big enough for the two of them to share without them being in the same room.

Wiping his feet on the mat, he quietly opened the sliding glass doors with the intent of racing upstairs to his room for a few hours until hunger drove him back down again. He hadn't managed to get more than one foot inside before Scott whipped his head around. The man's intense gaze bored into him. Kitt froze for a second before mentally shaking himself once more. He wasn't doing anything wrong. There was no reason for him to slink around and cower whenever Scott looked at him. He forced a nonchalance to his movements as he fully entered the house and slid the door closed behind him.

"You're up." He rolled his eyes while he still faced away from Scott. *How inane. Forget being fearful of Scott.* If Kitt didn't find alternative housing soon, he'd kill himself with embarrassment and save Emilio the trouble. "Did you sleep well?" He sent Scott a smile over his shoulder before turning to face him.

"Yeah, thanks." The man turned back to his game then twisted around to look at Kitt again. Scott was so big that he dwarfed the large chair. "Thanks for the iced tea and food. That was nice of you, but don't feel you have to feed me or anything."

Like Karen, Scott had blue eyes, except there was something more compelling about his. The color was that much deeper, almost navy. *Which is kind of poetic, given his job.* He couldn't help smiling at the errant thought—nor could he make himself look away. Instead of scuttling out of sight the way he'd intended, he stood staring at the guy, unable to think of a response. All the words that popped into his head seemed stupid. Then Scott narrowed his eyes and frowned. The angry look frightened Kitt. His heartbeat kicked up as he tried to think of what he'd done wrong.

"You're burned. Didn't you put on any sunscreen?"

Kitt blinked at the question for a few seconds before dropping his gaze to his arms and midriff. Yup, there was a tinge of red developing along his exposed skin. "Oh, I forgot." He felt stupid, and Emilio's taunting voice rang inside his head.

"You don't have the brains that God gave a goose. You couldn't survive one day without me."

He expected the same dismissive dressing down from Scott. No way a Navy SEAL ever forgot anything. What had Karen said her brother's motto was — *two is one and one is none*? Yeah, that sounded right. Kitt knew his own should be a perpetual facepalm emoji.

Scott didn't put him down for his mistake, however. Instead, the man said, "Do you have anything to put on that?" He jutted his very square jaw in the direction of Kitt's torso.

Kitt fidgeted. "Um, no."

Scott sighed and stood. "Come on." He walked over to the stairs and started climbing without waiting to see if Kitt followed. "Karen has some gunk with aloe in it that she uses for the kids. There must some left in the bathroom."

Kitt hesitated for a fraction of a second before hurrying after him. He didn't really question the why of it. Following Scott seemed the natural thing to do.

They trooped up to the second floor and into the communal bathroom off the hallway. When he'd used it before to shower, the space had felt roomy. Now, with Scott's large body occupying it, Kitt wasn't comfortable entering the whole way. He hovered mid-threshold, trying not to squirm or shuffle his feet, watching Scott rummage through the medicine cabinet. It was overflowing with all kinds of bottles and tubes.

Scott snatched one and held it out. "This is it. Karen swears by the stuff, and the twins always seem to stop fussing within seconds of her rubbing it on their burns. Of course," he continued, "the kids are getting too old for her to apply it—except for those spots that, you know, are hard to reach."

Kitt wasn't sure why he hesitated to take what was being offered. There was less than a foot between them. All he had to do was reach out, take the aloe and retreat to his bedroom, where he could strip off his shirt and ease his burn, which was starting to make itself known.

Scott didn't push the issue, either. They stood staring at each other, the man's lips pulled into a grim line. Then, before Kitt could get past his weird inertia, Scott broke the spell.

"Turn around and pull up your shirt so I can do your back. As short as that T-shirt is, you've got exposed skin the entire way around. You'll be miserable if you can't get this cream on all the spots you need it."

"Oh." That made sense. And yet it was hard for him to ward off a frisson of ambiguity while he did as he'd been told. He was good at obedience, though. Emilio had trained him well. It didn't make him stupid. Getting this close to a strange man, allowing him even superficial access to his body, took a big leap of trust. It was only the sure knowledge that Karen would never put him in harm's way that gave him the extra nudge he needed to give Scott his back.

No, that wasn't entirely true. As he stood facing the hallway and grabbed the bottom of his shirt, he had to admit to himself that there was something about this man that made him feel safe. There was solidness to Scott, a steadiness that had nothing to do with his size and more to do with the way the guy looked at him. There was no arrogance in his gaze, no threat or even demand. Instead, he radiated the kind of confidence one dreamt about in an alpha male who didn't require a heavy hand to get his way. And from everything Karen had said, Scott was also the type of man who took care of his own. Right at that moment, Kitt felt as if he fell into that category of someone Scott was looking after.

Kitt pulled his shirt off carefully, wincing as the fabric rubbed against his increasingly sensitive skin. Then he stood with his shoulders slightly hunched, waiting for... He wasn't sure what to expect. Certainly not the light, almost butterfly touch of Scott's fingertips. He applied the cream in a slow, constant swipe across the small of his back. To his sunburned skin, the aloe cream was cool. Kitt couldn't help shivering, his muscles rippling under the gentle assault. His breath caught, and he had to fight to steady it. Really, this was ridiculous. Scott's touch was practically clinical.

And oddly not. There was something almost sensual about it as those thick, blunt fingertips passed from one side of his torso to the other. Scott's movements paused, then resumed again with another application. This second round of caretaking was no less electrifying. Kitt's nerves tingled, goosebumps rose all over his body and his dick twitched in another minor awakening after nearly a year of terrified hiding. He was aware of Scott's breathing behind him, could feel warm breath tickling the back of his neck. But he didn't feel as if the man loomed. There was no predatory threat.

"Cute tattoo."

The observation startled Kitt. He shuddered out a breath before answering, "A rainbow to mark my first Pride." That reminded him of the heady times after he'd left home, the terror of being on his own warring with the exhilaration of finally being free to be who he was. To not hide. "I forget it's there, to be honest. I can't see it, you know?" He winced again, this time over his own silly remarks.

"I can understand that." Scott's tone wasn't mocking. "It was actually a smart place to put one. You only have to show it if you want to, and the small of the back ages well. No sagging rainbows in your future."

There was moment of silence that practically screamed 'awkward' before Scott took his fingers off Kitt's skin. He coughed once. "Sorry... I didn't mean to imply that you're going to age poorly or anything. It's, ah, just how skin is. You obviously take care of yourself, and I bet you'll age really well, and..." The man cursed. "Never mind. I'm babbling. You're all set back here." The tube of aloe appeared suspended over Kitt's shoulder. "I'll leave you to it."

Kitt only hesitated a couple of seconds before accepting the cream. He forced his feet to move out of the way and down the hall. "Thanks," he tossed over his shoulder, resisting the urge to watch Scott leave.

Then he hid in his room with the door shut, although from what, he wasn't sure. Really, who was he worried about—Scott or himself?

Chapter Three

Kitt spent a couple of hours in his bedroom, trying to calm himself with simple yoga exercises. It was difficult to do in the smallish space, especially because he was feeling the effects of his burn, making his skin tight and scratchy, despite the aloe cream he'd slathered on. If he gave himself even two seconds of free thought, he could still feel Scott's fingers on the small of his back. Because that was *so* not helping his efforts to chill, he kept forcing his mind back to focus on something else, like the memories of the sights and sounds of the sea.

With the window open, the soothing noise filtered in. But his concentration got shot to hell any time he heard Scott's muted footsteps and the low buzzing of voices from whatever the man was watching on TV. This house, while undeniably adorable, was like the set of *The Waltons* — one of the few shows his family had deemed wholesome enough for watching — with paper-thin walls and ceilings, it seemed. He wondered idly during one of his concentration lapses if Scott would bid him goodnight from down the hall.

"This is ridiculous." He breathed out and stood with a slight wince from his sunburn. His efforts at relaxing and putting Scott out of his mind had failed. He was no calmer than when he'd started, but he was hungry. *Time to make dinner*.

The idea that he had someone else to cook for made him smile as he left his room and headed downstairs. It was always more fun to share his food with others, and he was proud of his skills in the kitchen. As he did a mental tally of what he had for ingredients, he decided to make the beef stir-fry that he'd originally planned for that night. With the extra big mouth to feed, there would still be enough. He just wouldn't have any leftovers for the next day. That was fine, actually. Scott could take him shopping for more food in a couple of days. He stumbled a bit at the bottom of the stairs when a surge of domestic bliss hit him square in the solar plexus.

Kitt half-expected Scott to be right there, arms outstretched and ready to catch him. He frowned when that didn't prove to be the case. A quick glance confirmed that Scott wasn't anywhere on the first floor. The TV was turned off now, too. Sure that he hadn't heard Scott upstairs, Kitt headed over to the sliding glass doors that led to the deck and peered out. He spotted the man within a second, racing down the beach, bare-chested and wearing only cargo shorts and...*boots*? That seemed an odd choice, and as Karen had predicted, he was running suicides. Even from a distance, Kitt could see sweat gleaming on the man's skin, the glow from the setting sun giving it a tawny shade.

There were a lot of muscles on display, bunching and flexing with Scott's abrupt, speedy movements. It was impossible to look away. Kitt tried and failed, his fascination with all that raw power overwhelming his social graces or even his recent vow to stay off men for a good long while. Under the not-quite-pretext of fetching the jug of tea he'd set to brew in the sun earlier in the afternoon, he stepped out onto the deck and went to the railing. Now he was shamelessly ogling, and yet he couldn't make himself turn away. As Scott headed in his direction, he looked up, an unexpected move, although really Kitt should have realized that he could be seen as easily as he was watching. In the next second, Scott's feet flew out from under him and he landed hard on his ass. The fall was so quick that Kitt imagined he could hear the impact.

Knowing all too well how much alpha males hated anyone seeing their failures and weaknesses, Kitt abruptly turned away. He grabbed the jug and carried it back into the house. His nerves jangling more than ever, he set about the mundane task of making dinner, starting with sweetening and chilling the new batch of tea. Then he put rice on to cook, doubling his usual batch. By the time he was enmeshed in chopping vegetables, he'd calmed and had almost forgotten that Scott was outside until the sliding door opened. His heartbeat skipped before he made himself glance at the man. Really, if he was going to get this worked up over little things, his plan of sharing the house was doomed.

"Hi." That was all he got out before his spit dried because, Lord, now his view of Scott's sweaty body was completely unobstructed. The man stood in the living room, dressed only in his shorts, his skin glistening and his chest expanding with slightly quickened breaths. Given the amount of effort he'd been exerting, he should have been puffing like a locomotive. The man was obviously *very* fit. His slick skin highlighted every dip and curve of his impressive muscles. If there was an ounce of fat on the guy, it was hiding like Waldo.

Kitt returned his attention to the cutting board, happy to see that he hadn't cut off a finger during his distraction. "Dinner will be ready in about thirty minutes."

The sound of bare feet slapping against the tiled kitchen floor caught his attention before the scent of a man who'd worked out, mixed with the salty ocean air, hit his nose. "That's great, but remember, I don't expect you to cook for me."

Kitt waved that statement away without daring to shift his gaze again. "It's no bother. I was going to make this stir-fry for myself anyway. I'm really only making more rice than planned. I'm happy to do it," he added with a quick flick of his eyes. He couldn't resist. He flushed and hoped that his sunburn hid his reaction. It was ridiculous. He was acting like a high schooler.

"Well…um, thanks. I guess I should go take another shower. I'm pretty rank."

Not trusting his voice, Kitt merely nodded and concentrated on not hurting himself with the knife in his hand. He had to practically bite his tongue not to say something truly absurd such as 'don't bother on my account'. It wasn't until he heard Scott's foot hit the first step on the stairs that a question occurred to him and popped out of his mouth before he could stop it.

"Why were you running in boots?" He looked at the man with the side of his eyes.

Scott flashed a grin, making him look boyish. "It's an old SEAL trick. Makes it harder to do and works your muscles more, especially on sand."

"Oh." Kitt carefully trimmed the broccoli stems. "It's certainly effective." The facepalm emoji flashed before him. He closed his eyes, expecting...he didn't know what.

Scott just chuckled and continued to pound up the stairs. Kitt returned his full attention to the task at hand, wondering how he could possibly survive an evening with this man, let alone a couple of weeks.

* * * *

Scott stood under the beating spray of the shower, trying to rid himself of his renewed agitation from seeing Kitt again. One would have thought sprinting himself into exhaustion would have done the trick, but no. Whatever calm he'd induced with his exertion had been chased away by the disturbing appeal of the young man's domestic efforts on his behalf. He'd known even before Kitt had confirmed it that he was making dinner for the both of them. In the short time that he'd been acquainted with this kid, he'd learned that he had a generous heart and a drive for helping.

Kitt was also not one to find pleasure in another's mistakes. That much had been clear when he'd turned away from the deck railing instead of openly laughing after Scott had landed on his ass. And there had been no teasing of any kind once Scott had re-entered the house. Maybe that was the effect of living with abuse. Kitt didn't want to goad Scott into violence. If that were the case, it made him sad and angry all over again. Still, he was grateful to not have to speak of his ass-jarring fall in any way, especially as it had been caused purely by the sudden and alarming distraction of realizing Kitt was watching him. *What is it about this guy that turns me into a self-conscious, horny sixteen-year-old again?*

There was no satisfactory answer to that question, so he didn't try to give himself one. Instead, he did what he'd always done whenever he felt unwanted interest—banished it back to the corner of his mind from where it had come and shunned it. Given that a prolonged shower only served to pump more water into the septic system than was prudent, he finished quickly. And being a SEAL, he wasn't one to shy away from trouble. Wanting to run toward it was kind of an essential characteristic when becoming one. He could do this—have dinner with his house guest, then escape to his room. *No, no…retire.* Peace and quiet were going to be essential for getting the most out of his leave and lying in bed with a good book was the perfect way to spend the evening…except his mind flashed on something else that he might lie with. *Someone else.*

"Get your shit together, Carpenter," he muttered as he got dressed while studiously ignoring the giant bed in the middle of the small room. He deliberately put on a T-shirt because he hadn't missed Kitt's gaze roaming his chest and didn't want to be a tease—or a threat. It had been hard to tell if the kid's reaction had been one of interest or fear. The fact that he hadn't been able to tell was problematic. No way did he want to do anything that gave Kitt the wrong message. Better to play it safe all around.

The amazing smell of dinner hit him as he descended the stairs. He found Kitt plating up their food. The distribution was uneven by a large margin. It was as if a bear were going to share a meal with a mouse, and it was obvious who was what in that simile. *Or is it a metaphor?* English hadn't been his best subject. Math had been, however, and he didn't like how the numbers were adding up in this situation.

He frowned at the sight. "That can't be enough food for you."

Kitt glanced at him before scraping the last of the stir-fry onto what had to be Scott's plate. "Sure it is. I don't need much." Putting the empty pan on the stove, he reached into the silverware drawer to take out two forks. Then he started to grab the plates.

Scott stopped him with a gentle hold on his wrist. The simple contact was like an electric shock. He felt the jolt right down to his balls. So did Kitt. Scott could tell by the way the guy jerked at first. Or maybe that was again something more worrisome — fright rather than interest. The way Kitt stared at their physical connection with wide eyes wasn't particularly illuminating, either. Regardless, Scott knew he had to backpedal fast.

He pulled his hand away as if he'd been burned, which was sort of true on all kinds of weird levels. "Sorry," he said, without knowing exactly what he meant by it. "I appreciate getting the lion's share of the food, but I hate the idea that you might go hungry later on. Why don't we put some of mine back in the pan? You can save it, just in case."

Kitt raised his gaze to stare at him directly, took a noticeably deep breath and said, "Nope, I'm good." With that, he picked up the plates and hurried over to the dining table. It was already set so they would sit opposite each other. A pitcher of iced tea was in the middle and two tall glasses with ice were waiting to be filled. Kitt took one of the chairs and waited with his hands on his lap.

Surprised at his companion's reaction, Scott joined him, careful to make every movement slow and non-threatening, because despite his firm refusal, Kitt looked uneasy. "Okay, I'm going to trust that you know your own needs." Without asking, he grabbed Kitt's glass and filled it before doing the same with his own.

Determined to make dinner as quick and painless as possible, Scott dug into his food. The first bite had him groaning. "Oh my God, this is amazing." He spoke with his mouth full, despite his upbringing, unable to hold back his delight. Any regret he might have had was wiped away at Kitt's reaction.

The man beamed. There was no other word for it, albeit in a uniquely shy way that was adorable. "I'm glad you like it."

Before shoveling in another mound of beef, vegetables and rice, he said, "How could I not? I mean, I eat out a lot because I can't cook worth a damn, and this is as good as anything a restaurant could put out."

"That's kind of you to say, although I did learn from my grandparents and they ran a diner back home." He scooped up a small amount with his fork and ate it almost daintily—wrapping his lips around the tines and sliding the morsels into his mouth. There was something almost erotic about the simple movements.

Because watching Kitt was bad for his digestion, Scott downed some iced tea before focusing on his plate. "Where are you from?" *There, small talk. No reason to get freaked out.*

"Omaha."

"Oh, yeah? I know someone in the Teams from Lincoln."

Kitt flashed a grin. "That's a lovely college town. I visited there once."

Scott nodded, happy to stick to safe topics. "He went to the University. Go Big Red." When Kitt only blinked at him in obvious confusion, he added, "You know, the football team?"

"Oh, right." He shrugged as he took another forkful. "I'm not really into sports."

Okay, so that eliminated a topic of discussion. Searching around for another safe one, Scott went back to food. "So, you grew up learning to cook. What made you go into hairdressing?"

Now Kitt's face morphed into a bright smile. "I've always loved playing with hair. I used to style and even try to color my sister's Barbie dolls."

"Really? She must have enjoyed that."

Kitt's face fell and he stared at his plate. "No, she didn't. She told our father and he…put a stop to it." He brought his hand up to that ugly bruise on his face for a second before dropping it onto his lap again.

Scott tightened his fingers around his fork and balled his other hand into a fist without conscious thought. It didn't take any imagination to get how Kitt's father had accomplished his goal. The idea of anyone putting his hands on this sweet boy like that was infuriating. And having come from an abusive father, it was easy to see how Kitt had fallen into another relationship based on the same kind of 'love'. It was an assumption that was hard to deny.

Because it was impossible for him to go back in time and fix either of those problems, he decided the best thing he could do for Kitt was keep the present as stress-free as possible. "Well, my sister says you're amazing at what you do. She's a hard person to please, so that's high praise in my book."

Kitt rewarded his efforts with another smile, and this time it was warm and clearly genuine. "She's a lovely person, and her bark is worse than her bite. I've always found her to be generous and patient."

Scott paused mid-bite. "Seriously? I mean, generous fits, but patient?" He snorted. "Karen has always operated at warp speed and hates that everyone else has to work to keep up."

"I expect we see different sides of her. I can't imagine she would give her younger brother much quarter."

Scott grinned. "A military expression...and perfectly apt." He drank more tea, refilled both their glasses, then said, "How did you know I was younger?"

Kitt rolled his eyes, an expression that made him look carefree. "She kept talking about her 'baby' brother. I imagined you were this little kid or something. Then she showed me a picture of you two together and you were like this giant—and grizzly to boot, full beard and everything."

Scott scratched at his cheek, where stubble was coming in. He'd done only a cursory shave when he'd returned stateside, and that had been a few days ago. "I spend a lot of time in places where not only is soap and water in short supply, but manliness is measured in part by facial hair." He scratched some more. "I need to shave tomorrow. I don't like having stubble or a beard when it's not essential for the job."

Kitt actually sniffed when he said, "I bet you use one of those store-bought disposable razors."

Scott shrugged. "Doesn't everybody?"

"Not those of us who know how to use a straight one, not that I personally need to shave very often." He stroked his smooth cheek, a move that Scott tracked like a hawk.

He made himself look away. "You mean one of those old-fashioned straight razors with a strop?" When Kitt nodded, he added, "Shit, as good as I am with a blade, I'd be worried I'd cut my own throat." He bit his tongue immediately afterward, realizing his reference highlighted how lethal he was. So much for keeping the conversation light.

Kitt surprised him by looking smug. "It's a skill that can be mastered. I happen to have learned it at hairdressing school." He paused. "I, um, brought my kit with me. I'd be happy to give you a shave...if you'd like," he added in a soft tone then lowered his gaze.

That look of vulnerability made Scott want to do whatever it took to bring the smile back to that lovely face. "Hey, you know, I'd like that. I've had it done in other countries, actually, where it's more common. And it is a much closer shave than what I can achieve in the shower."

It was the right thing to say. Kitt was now beaming again. "How about tomorrow morning?"

"Perfect."

The rest of dinner was easier after that, albeit a quick affair. Scott wasn't one to linger over his meals and was practically licking the plate within minutes. "That was great, thanks." He finished his drink then stood with his place setting in hand. Because Kitt was also done, he reached for that one, as well.

Kitt jumped to his feet. "Let me do that." He held out his hands.

Scott pulled the items out of reach. "No, sir. You cooked, I clean. That's the rule in this house. Always has been, so blame my grammy if you must."

He didn't wait for a reply, merely turned toward the kitchen. "Why don't you put on the TV? Find something you'll like, because I'm going to go up and read in bed for the rest of the evening."

"Oh, that's okay. I'm sure there's a game of some sort that you'd like to see. I don't watch much TV, anyway."

Scott didn't believe that statement for a moment and figured it was one more way that Kitt was trying to appease him. He decided he needed to stay firm, and if that meant spending more time with his guest, so be it. Hiding in his bedroom was a cowardly retreat anyway.

Placing the dirty dishes in the sink, he called over his shoulder, "Naw, I'm done with sports for the day. Put something on, and I'll come join you when I'm done...if that's all right," he added. No sense in crowding the guy, even with good intentions.

There was a pause before Kitt answered. "Sure."

It wasn't the most enthusiastic response, but within seconds, something was playing on the flat screen that contained a fair amount of construction sounds. A quick glance told Scott that Kitt had turned on some kind of home renovation show. It wasn't what Scott had expected and probably something Kitt had thought Scott would like, but there was only so much overanalyzing and fretting he could do about this situation. He put the worry out of his mind and got busy stacking the dishwasher.

The activity reminded him of how, in his grandmother's time, everything had been done by hand. He could remember the first time she'd had him kneel on a chair to reach the sink when he was little. Everyone had been expected to pull their own weight in her household, and she hadn't gone in for fancy machines, as she'd called them. Of course, his mother and Karen had redone the kitchen once Grammy had died. It was a whole lot easier, but he was still grateful for the lessons and the responsibilities. They helped him in the field, actually—the best training in the world.

While he cleared and wiped the dining table, he kept his gaze off Kitt. That didn't mean he wasn't completely aware of the guy's location and every move. It seemed impossible to not be. Kitt was curled up on the sofa, quiet and non-intrusive, yet he might as well have been beating a drum the way Scott's senses were keyed into him. There wasn't enough housework to keep Scott busy, so he killed two birds with one stone by deciding to microwave some popcorn. He had to search well into the back of a cupboard to find it but felt a sense of victory when he did. It was a pretty constant staple for his family, and score... It was the kind with butter and salt, none of that 'healthy' stuff that Karen liked. The smell of it by the time the microwave dinged had him salivating. He dumped it into a bowl and carried it over to the sitting area.

Kitt was still curled into the far corner of the couch, his gaze glued to the TV. The look on his face when Scott put popcorn on the coffee table made Scott feel as if he'd just donated the guy his kidney or something.

"That's so nice of you!"

It was possible Scott's cheeks heated in reaction, but he decided to ignore that because it was too embarrassing. He *never* blushed. "I figured we could both use a treat. Not that it's anything like those cookies you baked." He snapped his fingers. "Damn, I'd forgotten. Would you like those instead? Or in addition to?"

Kitt gnawed at his lower lip. "No, thanks. This is plenty." So saying, he dug into the bowl and pulled out a fistful of popcorn. Then he darted his eyes back to the screen and kept them there as if the screen held the very secret of life.

With the hope of making his guest feel less like an interloper, Scott made the decision to hang out for a while, but where to sit? The show that Kitt had chosen was entertaining enough, and having slept most of the day, it wasn't as though Scott was sleepy. The idea that he'd lie in bed reading wasn't realistic, either. He could feel the restlessness prowling inside him, unabated by exercise, a quick jerk-off session in the shower or a full stomach.

Maybe watching a woman sweat her way through a demolition project would prove distracting. Her male partner was equally compelling in an obviously deliberate way. Seriously, who did demo shirtless? But he wasn't going to go *there*. Besides, he would be fooling himself to insist that either of the show's hosts held a candle to the kind of distraction that was currently sitting curled like a kitten on the sofa.

If he were smart, he'd park his ass on the nearby chair. However, that would put him too far away from the bowl of popcorn and would too easily be seen by Kitt as deliberately trying to stay away from him. Knowing that it could be misinterpreted as disgust rather than what it really was, he couldn't do it to the kid. That bruised cheek and the wary look in his eyes were like a gut punch every time Scott saw them. The last thing he wanted to do was cause more anxiety. Kitt could use a relaxing night. They both could.

So, Scott scooped a handful of popcorn and plunked himself down on the opposite end of the couch. Immediately, he became even more aware of Kitt's proximity. The sweet scent of the aloe cream caught his attention to a degree it hadn't before. Out of the corner of his eye, Kitt's delicate profile held his focus, even as the woman on the TV stripped down to a skimpy tank top. Her breasts spilled over in a way that surely OSHA wouldn't have approved, given the various particles flying through the air with each swing of her sledgehammer. Scott tossed pieces of his snack one-by-one into his mouth as he struggled to keep his attention on the intended form of entertainment instead of where his unruly mind kept insisting on returning.

It didn't work. As Kitt finished eating his current handful of popcorn, he stuck his forefinger into his mouth and slowly sucked off the residue of butter and salt. Scott knew that was the intent because everyone did the same thing, including himself. There was something, however, about the way Kitt slowly cleaned each digit that became more riveting than the television show. Not even the bouncing breasts of the co-host had the same allure, and damn if Scott didn't try to change that fact. He kept forcing his gaze back to the television, only to find his focus shifting sideways with each little slurpy pop Kitt made.

Despite the air-conditioning humming away, Scott's body heated. He imagined how great an ice-cold bottle of beer would be but didn't have the energy to get back up. It was weird, as if he'd deflated, felt boneless, and yet at the same time restless energy churned inside him. Part of the feeling was familiar. He always had pent-up energy and a sense that he was slacking whenever he was back in the States. That wasn't the whole of it, though. There was something simmering underneath which could only be described as sexual need.

I need to get laid.

His gaze darted toward Kitt before he could stop the impulse. He clenched his fingers and wished that somehow a bottle of beer would magically appear and soothe his heated blood. Or maybe a piano could fall on his head and knock him out with ruthless efficiency. *Either way, problem solved.*

No sooner had the ridiculous thought entered his head, than Kitt stood abruptly. "I'm going to get a glass of iced tea," he said, without looking directly as Scott.

"Would you like one...or a beer, maybe? There was some in the fridge when I arrived."

Kitt was on the move before Scott was able to answer. He called after him, "A beer would be great, but you don't have to wait on me." He half-rose as Kitt literally waved away the concern.

"It's no bother. I'm here already for myself."

Deciding that arguing the point was ridiculously unnecessary, Scott turned back to the television. Staring at Kitt as he went about his domestic efforts would be creepy. So, he pretended to be fascinated by a woman hawking toilet paper until a cold bottle of beer appeared in front of his face.

He grabbed it, trying and failing to avoid skimming the backs of Kitt's fingers. "Thanks." He chugged half of it down before Kitt had been able to return to his spot on the other end of the couch.

His houseguest's body language rang alarm bells as he curled away from Scott, as close to the arm as he could get. It didn't take a psychology degree to realize that Kitt was leery about a man drinking, so Scott slowed down, sipping the rest of his beer in small mouthfuls. He also made a point of making a show of relaxing. When the program they were watching segued into one about women acting crazy as they searched for the perfect wedding dress, Kitt reached for the remote.

"Sorry... This is obviously nothing you want to watch." The apology made little sense, as if Kitt had control over the cable scheduling.

"It's fine. Really," he added when Kitt raised his eyebrows. "There's nothing else on that I know of that I'd prefer, and actually, I helped Karen pick out her gown."

"No way!" Kitt's expression turned into open skepticism, but he was so obviously delighted that Scott was glad he'd made the confession.

He took a quick swig of his beer as he nodded. "I did. I was home on leave, and she wanted a masculine viewpoint. My job was to try to look at her as if I were her husband seeing his bride for the first time walking down the aisle. It was kind of creepy and uncomfortable, honestly. I had to imagine another woman's head on her shoulders, but she did go with my suggestion. Ben teared up when he saw her, so I guess it was the right call. Of course," he added, "he would have reacted the same way if she'd worn a sack..."

Kitt turned toward Scott. "I've seen the pictures, and it was perfect for her. You did an excellent job."

Scott couldn't help grinning, stupidly happy with the compliment. "Yeah? Good to know I have options when I retire from the Navy. Maybe I can get my own show," he added in a teasing tone, because the idea that he could spend hours shepherding stressed-out women through the bridal shops was ludicrous.

Kitt didn't think so, apparently. "You could totally do that. Straight women, and gay men would tune in just to get a look at you once a week." His eyes widened, and he snapped his lips shut with a grimace. He shifted his gaze back to the television. "I mean, you know how shallow people are, and if you did it shirtless, well..." Kitt gulped down some of his iced tea. "I'll shut up now."

Scott chuckled, stupidly touched by the ardent pitch of his marketability. "Thanks," was all he said, because he didn't want to make Kitt any more uncomfortable than he seemed to be doing already.

It was surprisingly easy to sink into companionable silence, other than the occasional shared groan when one of the women made an obviously bad choice. When his first beer was drained, Scott didn't feel the need for another. Instead, he slouched into his corner, dangling the empty bottle from his finger and thumb and letting his muscles relax. By the time the show ended, he was yawning. Jet lag was getting to him, his body thoroughly confused about what time zone he was in. It was something he was used to and usually fought against to force himself to adapt to the local rhythm. This night, however, his eyelids started to droop with increasing frequency. That, along with his loud yawns, made it impossible to hide his desperate need for more sleep.

He stood and stretched, careful not to make his movements sudden. Kitt had obviously become comfortable in his presence, and he didn't want to do anything to jeopardize that. When the boy flicked his gaze over to him, Scott grinned.

"Apparently, it's past my bedtime. I'm going to go turn in. If you're staying in for the night, I'll check to make sure everything's locked up."

Kitt gave him a shy smile. "Thanks, I'd appreciate that. And good night. I promise I'll be quiet."

"No worries. I'm a light sleeper when I need to be. Otherwise, very little will disturb me." He felt as if he should say more, do more, yet there was clearly nothing. So, he rinsed his bottle and put it in the recycling bin, did a perimeter check and headed for the upstairs. With one foot on the bottom step, he turned toward the living room.

"Good night, Kitt."

His houseguest turned his head to look at him from over his shoulder. "Good night, Scott. I'm glad you're here."

That last bit was said in the direction of the television, and with such a quiet voice that Scott could almost believe he'd imagined it. Nevertheless, he felt ten feet tall as he headed for bed.

Chapter Four

The nightmare ended as they always did — with Kitt bolting upright in bed, a silent scream on his lips. He heaved harsh breaths as he tried to rein in his terror. Despite the air conditioner pumping cool air into the room, a coat of sweat covered his tight, sunburned skin. His stomach threatened to toss his evening meal and hugging it with shaky arms wasn't helping. It never did, but he had no other way to deal with it. The bad dreams had started before he'd run from Emilio, and silently trying to hold himself together had become his only avenue. His man had hated being woken in the night and there had been no way to explain why Kitt was in such a state, not to the demon driving the frightening images.

The fact that he was now alone hadn't quite sunk in to his inner child, so he didn't stray from his ingrained reaction to waking in that manner He was grateful that it was only a nightmare and not a portent of how his day might begin or end. And there was something more that helped. Down the hall was a man who he trusted against all odds, or even reason, to be there to protect him. Still, he didn't want to disturb Scott out of courtesy, if nothing else. Remaining silent, he slipped out of bed and went to the door. He cracked it open and listened. Hearing nothing, he went into the hall and padded downstairs as quietly as he knew how.

His goal was to reach the sliding doors to the deck. He'd done this before, standing on the threshold, staring out at the moonlit sea, listening to the calming sounds of waves breaking. This night, however, he felt emboldened enough to step outside. It wasn't only the hope that he was safe in this tucked-away place... Scott was here now and Kitt was sure that if he let out a scream, the man would come charging to his rescue. The night air was chilly, his sleeveless tank and gym shorts no match for it, but he didn't want to go back inside to find his jacket or grab a blanket. The more moving around he did, the greater the risk of waking Scott. The man had been so obviously exhausted when he'd retired early.

So he stood by the railing of the deck, hugging himself against the chill, letting the magic of the setting chase away the remnants of the nightmare and allowing himself to be soothed. But with the lowering of his tension, the near hopelessness of his situation consumed him. Tears pooled, then slid past his eyes and down his cheeks. He didn't bother to wipe them away, allowing them to fall unchecked as he gave in to the sadness consuming him. *Why not?* There was no one to see or hear him. He didn't have to feel pathetic in his fear for his future.

"Hey."

The quiet word startled him, but only for a half-second. He knew who it was and recognized that there was no anger in the tone, only concern.

That didn't mean he wasn't embarrassed to be discovered weeping on the deck in the middle of the night. He had some pride. Hastily swiping at his face, he turned around and tried to smile. "Hi, I'm sorry. Did I wake you?"

Scott stood just beyond the sliding doors, his hair rumpled, cheeks stubbly, wearing a worn T-shirt and boxers that invited perusal. Even with the throw blanket from the couch slung over his arm, there was a lot of the large man on display. Kitt was careful to keep his gaze on the man's face.

Scott shrugged as he approached. "No. I was already up, just reading in bed. My internal clock is flunky, so first I couldn't keep my eyes open then couldn't stay asleep." He shrugged again. "I wanted to make sure you were all right." He got closer. "Obviously not."

Sensing more tears were spilling over, Kitt wiped at both cheeks with impatience. "I'm fine." When Scott stared at him, he amended, "It was only a bad dream. Nothing to worry about."

He turned to gaze at the ocean once more, wishing Scott would return to the house and leave him to his misery, and at the same time hoping he would stay. The conflicting desires were disturbing, and they made no sense. *God, why am I so stupid?*

The weight of the blanket fell onto his shoulders. "Here, put this on. You're shivering." There was a gruffness to Scott's tone that sent a frisson of alarm through Kitt until the man's sure touch settled the material around his arms. The obvious kindness behind the effort gave him comfort.

Kitt gathered the ends, ignoring how even the soft fleece irritated his burned skin. "Thanks. I wasn't thinking. It was so hot earlier."

Scott snorted as he stood beside Kitt at the railing, his big body radiating enough heat that the blanket was almost superfluous. "The shore can be cool at night, even at the height of summer. And nothing gives you the shivers more than a sunburn."

Kitt dared to flick a glance Scott's way. "You don't seem to be bothered by the temperature." He could have bitten his tongue the second the words were out of his mouth. Making small talk was a mistake. Better to urge the man to go back to bed so that Kitt could be alone with his misery.

Scott leaned on the railing. "My engine's always run a little hot. I prefer the cold. You'd hear plenty of complaining from me if this were August."

"It must be difficult for you to be fighting in such warm countries then." Again, that facepalm emoji flashed before his eyes. The last thing a military person on leave would want to be reminded of was deployment to a war zone. Maybe being so clueless was a good thing. Scott would make his excuses now and leave.

No such luck. Scott put his chin onto his arm and kept staring at the ocean. "I go where I'm needed. And while we do train for winter warfare, I won't get to use it much until Iceland develops a terrorism problem, I guess."

A giggle popped out before Kitt could stop it. He slammed his hand over his mouth and looked at Scott in order to apologize.

But Scott's head was already turned in his direction. "I don't mean to make light of such a serious matter."

His lips quirked. "Actually, yes I do. Humor is one of the ways my teammates and I get through the worst of it." He paused. "Laughing is better than crying."

Kitt found that smiling back wasn't hard. "That's true. Thanks for helping me get out of my nightmare funk." As he said the words, he realized it was true. His spirits were lifted, the terrors that had woken him fading in the background.

Scott straightened. "I'm glad I didn't make things worse. I wasn't sure you'd welcome the company, but I'm here if you'd like a chance to talk about it. If you *want*. Sometimes dreams are a spillover for something more serious. Leaving them to fester is not a good idea." Scott shook his head. "Listen to me, like I'm a therapist or something."

"You're not wrong," Kitt allowed. "You don't have to be Freud to get my dreams, to understand where they are coming from."

Scott said nothing for a long time. He stayed unmoving beside him, gazing out at the sea. "I love the ocean. There's something about it that calls to me — the way it looks and sounds and even smells. When I was a kid, coming here was like a way to rid myself of whatever was bothering me. It was more than fun in the sun. My own personal medicine."

"That's what Karen said too, that this place wasn't just somewhere secluded, that it would help me heal and give me time and space to get my life back on track."

Scott let some time slip by before responding. "Some asshole did a real number on you."

Tightness filled his chest. Pushing past it, Kitt made himself talk. "At first, Emilio was everything I thought I wanted. He made me feel safe and desirable. Special.

He complimented me about everything. Then, one night when he had to work late, I went out dancing at a club with some other boys. I hadn't made any real friends back home, and it was so nice to spend time with dudes my age. We had fun. That's all. I didn't hit on anyone and rebuffed the guys that approached me. I told them I was in a relationship and didn't cheat.

"I'd called to let Emilio know I was going to be late getting home. He hadn't picked up, but I'd left a voicemail. I thought if he minded, he'd call back and tell me. I would have left if he had asked. When I got home, he…" Kitt took a deep breath. "He was so angry and called me ungrateful. Called me stupid. Called me a slut." His voice caught on the last word. "It was like he was a completely different person."

Scott didn't say anything, simply stood beside him, a steady presence while Kitt gathered his courage to continue.

"By the time he got around to actually hitting me, I thought I deserved it." He curled his fingers around the blanket and leaned against the railing.

"No one deserves to be hit. You didn't do anything wrong, and even if you had, your boyfriend had no right to lash out physically."

Kitt worried his lower lip. "I know." Saying the words, meaning them, didn't quite do the trick of banishing the feelings of guilt and inadequacy.

Scott shifted his stance and before Kitt realized what he intended, he put his hand on Kitt's shoulder. Large as it was, it sat gently on him, a firm comfort without being dominating. "It will be easier to believe it the longer you stay away from him. Someday, you'll meet a guy who will show you how it should really be—a nice man who will treat you with kindness and respect."

Kitt allowed himself a brief moment to imagine that Scott would be that guy before he ruthlessly crushed the fantasy. *He's not for me.* "Are you sure you're straight?" He'd meant it as a joke, as a reminder to himself that this man was unattainable, if for no other reason.

Because Scott still had his hand on him, he was aware of the slight jerk. Then Scott let go entirely and put physical distance between them by turning toward the sliding doors. "Yeah, but I've got Karen for a sister, remember? And although you never got a chance to meet our mother and grandmother, she's the proverbial acorn, believe me. All three of them schooled me on the right way to treat women. I figure the same rules apply to every relationship."

His voice got more distant, and Kitt didn't have to see that the man had stepped inside the house. "I'm going to head back to bed. Are you okay?"

"I'm fine." Kitt made his voice steady and strong. "Really. Thanks for the blanket and the advice."

"You're welcome, although really neither of those things was much."

"More than you'll ever know," he replied softly to the retreating footsteps.

* * * *

Kitt opened his eyes slowly, squinting against the bright sunlight and wiping drool that had dried at the corner of his mouth. For a few seconds, he didn't understand where he was before remembering how he'd curled up on the chaise, wrapped in the blanket

Scott had brought him. He'd fallen asleep, obviously, but he couldn't remember what he'd dreamed, so it must have been benign, the nightmares banished for the rest of the night. For a few seconds, he lay on his side, watching the waves crash against the rocks and listening to the screeching of gulls overhead. It was a rather pleasant way to wake, actually.

The heat of the morning was already making him overly warm, so he pushed the cover away as he rolled onto his back. Then he sat up and stretched, swinging his legs toward the house and putting his bare feet on the deck. The first thing he noticed was Scott over in the kitchen. The man was working at the stove top, cooking something in a frying pan. Guilt rose within him, an automatic reaction upon seeing someone else doing his job. He should be the one making breakfast. But even as the thought crossed his mind, Scott looked over and saw him. The broad smile he shot in Kitt's direction chased away any concern. Regardless of how Kitt felt about the situation, Scott clearly didn't mind being stuck with making his own breakfast. A bit self-conscious, Kitt grinned back and gave a little wave.

He made himself stand and tried to act natural. There was nothing to be gained by continuing to be shy or awkward around his unexpected housemate. He folded the blanket before sliding the doors open and stepping inside the cool house. "Good morning." His voice held nothing of his feelings, which was a relief. He sauntered toward the kitchen, tossing the blanket onto the couch as he went. The mingled scents of coffee and eggs hit his nose.

"I hope you like scrambled eggs," Scott called out, his concentration on the frying pan. "It's about all I know how to make."

Kitt tucked a few strands of hair behind his ear as he approached, sure he looked a mess, given how he'd spent the remainder of the night — not that it seemed to matter to Scott in the least. "Sure. Thanks for making them."

Scott shrugged, still staring at the pan. "No sweat. I took my run earlier and was starving after my shower. I hope I didn't disturb you."

Kitt stopped by the dining counter. "No, not at all. Did you run on the beach?" When Scott nodded, he frowned. "Huh, I didn't hear you come out on the deck."

Now Scott did look up. His face was lit with amusement. "Navy SEAL, remember? I'm very good at stealth."

Kitt giggled. "Oh, right." He might have stood there, staring and grinning like an idiot, except his bladder intruded. "Um, excuse me a second."

He hurried to the downstairs half-bath and took care of his immediate need. Then he made the mistake of looking in the mirror while he washed his hands. "Yikes," he muttered, because his hair *was* a disaster. Worse, there was a checkered imprint from the chaise's weave on the cheek he'd been sleeping on. He really wanted to dash upstairs and take a shower, but his stomach rumbled. Not to mention that it would be rude to let Scott's food get cold while Kitt prettied himself.

"As if it matters what I look like," he reminded himself in a low voice.

Still, he washed his face and used his fingers as a comb before returning to the kitchen. Scott was already plating the eggs. "You didn't have to go to such trouble," Kitt said while heading for the coffee pot. He filled a mug and went for the cream in the refrigerator.

What had seemed like a lot of food when it had been only for himself now appeared sparse. Provisions were already dwindling rapidly with two of them eating—even after twenty-four hours—especially given that one of them had the appetite of ten men.

"It was no trouble, seriously."

When Kitt emerged from the fridge, he was surprised to find Scott practically on top of him. The big man took up a lot of room, the toaster had just popped up more slices and it was right by the refrigerator door. Kitt tried to step around him, but of course, Scott tried to give him room at the same time, causing them to come face-to-face again. They did the inside version of the 'sidewalk shuffle' that inevitably led to an awkward logjam, which Scott ended in a novel way—by grabbing Kitt by the waist, lifting his feet off the floor, whirling him around then setting him down. The maneuver was over in two seconds, leaving Kitt breathless with a little laugh.

Scott grabbed the slices of toast and tossed them onto a plate. "Sorry… That's the SEAL in me, again. I'm always looking for the quickest, best solution to any problem." He trained his gaze on Kitt. "I hope I didn't make you uncomfortable. I've done the same to other family members in the past. This kitchen's always been too small."

Kitt clutched the carton of cream to his chest, trying not to blush. "It was fine. No worries at all." Flustered, he doctored his coffee, then grabbed it and his plate of food. It was easy to spot which was his, because while it had a generous amount of eggs on it, the other one held a mountain of them.

Scott slathered butter on the toast. "Let's eat outside."

"Oh, that's a wonderful idea." Kitt juggled his mug and plate to grab utensils and napkins for them both. Scott was right on his heels as he headed back to the deck. Somehow, the man managed to carry two plates and a mug and still open the sliding doors to the deck. His thick arm brushed past Kitt's when he did so. A shiver went through Kitt and it wasn't caused by the sensitivity of his burn. He let Scott pick his spot first, and no surprise, the man chose the one where the sun shone brightest, giving Kitt the shaded area.

They sat quietly while the sun rose, eating their breakfast. The eggs were good and any meal that he hadn't had to cook himself was a treat. The coffee was delicious too, and it was all so lovely that Kitt had no trouble putting aside his shyness and worry and simply enjoyed the moment. Scott scarfed his food down with dizzying speed before sitting back with a sigh.

The man sipped his coffee and gazed out over the ocean. "It's going to be a beautiful day. I hate spending it indoors for even a moment, but we need to lay in more supplies. At the rate I'm going, I'll be eating the cupboard bare within another day. Once you're finished with breakfast, we should make a run to the store."

Kitt nodded as he chewed and swallowed. "Sure." The idea of leaving the sanctuary of the house gave him a moment's pause before he was able to squelch it. There was nothing to fear. Emilio had no idea where he was, and even if he somehow magically appeared by the frozen food section to accost him, Kitt would be more than fine. He would have Scott nearby, his own personal bodyguard. And while he was sure it would be all right to suggest instead that Scott go on his own, the idea didn't sit well with him. Hiding away in this cozy house was not an option for spending the rest of his life. *Best to get back out there now when I know I'm safe.*

Finishing the last of his food, he said, "I just need to shower and…I promised you a shave."

Scratching at his stubbly chin, Scott said, "That's right. It can wait, though."

Kitt shook his head. "No, let's do it this morning before we leave. You'll feel better for it. I know how itchy growing a new beard can be. It's fine if that's your goal, but if you want to be clean-shaven, best to get on it early. We can do it right out here, in fact."

"Oh, yeah?" Scott slouched. "You mean while I sit in this chair?"

"No, on the chaise. I can tip your head back that way."

Scott popped to his feet. "Great, I'll clean up while you shower and meet you back here when you're ready."

Kitt joined him and grabbed for the plates. "No, I'll take care of the dishes. You cooked, after all. House rules, remember?"

"No, it's fine." Scott firmly tugged everything out of Kitt's hands. "I don't mind, and the sooner you're ready, the better for me, right?" His quick smile was impossible to resist. And his allure was frighteningly so.

Kitt didn't even try. Letting go, he said, "Okay. Thanks." As there was nothing more to say, he abruptly went into the house and raced up the stairs.

He practically panted as he gathered his clean clothing from his room, and his breathlessness had nothing to do with physical exertion. No, his racing heart and strained lungs were a direct result of Scott's proximity. No matter how hard he tried to ignore his reaction to the man, his body just would not get with the program—and that included his dumb dick. A glance downward confirmed that an erection pressed against the soft cotton of his briefs. *God, really?* His libido had been in hiding for so long. Why couldn't it have stayed there for a little while longer?

Embarrassed and annoyed in equal measure, Kitt placed the bundle of clean clothing strategically in front of the bulge, just in case Scott decided to come upstairs before Kitt made it to the bathroom. He paused only so long as was necessary to grab towels from the hallway cupboard before secluding himself and his rampant arousal behind a closed door. It was ridiculous how relieved he felt when he was sure he was alone again. He quickly stripped down, ignoring the rasping against his poor, reddened skin, and turned on the shower. He also deliberately ignored his bobbing cock as he got under the spray. The distracting pain of the water hitting his sunburn was very welcome, but even that didn't cause his erection to flag. By the time he'd finished washing his hair, he'd come to accept that this pesky renewal of life wasn't going to simply go away on its own.

"You are being ridiculous!" he admonished his penis as if it were some sentient being that could be reasoned with. "I don't have time for this nonsense. Shut it down."

Of course, his words had no effect, and neither did his efforts at mentally willing it away. In the end, he had to do the obvious—which only took a few quick strokes. The intensity of the orgasm caught him by surprise. He stumbled on a gasp and nearly landed on his ass. By the time he'd regained his footing, he was actually laughing. There was some combination of the absurdity of it all and the relief at knowing that he wasn't permanently broken by his experience with his former lover. As he stood panting under the spray, he found that he felt lighter, happy even, as if his climax had purged some awful thing that had been clogging his mind.

Finishing the shower quickly, Kitt dried, dressed and otherwise made himself presentable for the rest of the day. There had been a tough moment as he'd spread more aloe on his sunburn when he recalled with a sudden and vivid memory of how it had felt when Scott had soothed his lower back. His dick had tried to rally, but this time he'd wrangled it under control. And despite his being intent on giving Scott a 'proper' shave, he'd used his daily safety razor on small patches of wispy stubble trying to sprout on his face.

He returned to his room to retrieve the leather satchel that contained his hairdressing tools. It had been one of the few things he'd been able to grab before fleeing the apartment he'd shared with Emilio. This equipment was expensive and his ticket to re-starting his life. Nestled inside were his prized straight razor and other gear needed for a shave. He didn't have any shaving cream, however, so on his way downstairs, he grabbed the aloe from the bathroom — a decent-enough substitute — as well as a bottle of witch hazel on the assumption that Scott didn't have any aftershave with him.

He found the kitchen spotless and Scott back outside, reclining on the chaise. The man was utterly relaxed and so obviously in command of his space that it was an impressive sight. But the moment Kitt's feet hit the final step, there was a noticeable stiffening of the man's body before he raised his sunglasses and turned in Kitt's direction. Even at a distance, Scott's stare had the power to make Kitt's belly quiver — not from fear, though. The resurgence of his sexual desire was not as frightening this time, although still very inconvenient. Fortunately, he wore a long T-shirt and snug jeans. His cock had nowhere to go so it simply ached, and Kitt was determined to ignore it. He needed a steady hand for what he'd come down to do.

Pasting what he hoped was a mostly genuine breezy smile on his face, he headed for the deck. He placed his armful of stuff on the table and gestured for Scott to stay where he was when the man started to rise. "Just hang tight. I need to heat a wet towel to soften your whiskers." It was rather gratifying when Scott instantly obeyed and also rewarded him with another of those smiles.

Back in the kitchen, Kitt found it relatively easy to go into professional mode. He was passionate about his job and confident that he did it extremely well. He soaked a dishtowel under the faucet before placing it into a bowl and heating it in the microwave, rather pleased with himself at figuring out how to use what was available to him. *SEALs aren't the only ones who can improvise with what they have.* When he returned to the deck, he found Scott right where he'd left him and had no trouble getting the towel wrapped around the man's face. The tingle Kitt felt at the brief contact only distracted him for a moment.

"How's that?" he asked as he pressed the cloth in place. "Not too hot?"

Scott murmured some kind of reassurance, and like a dentist, Kitt had become accustomed to interpreting his clients' incoherent replies. Satisfied that all was well, he started the process of prepping his gear.

Because it had been a while since he'd used the razor, he placed his ceramic barber hone on the table and got to work. Everything he had was top of the line because his clients deserved the best. He knew that a razor could last generations, not that he had much hope of having children to pass it down to. In his more wistful and naïve moments, he'd dreamed of getting married and raising a family. Now, it was hard to imagine ever finding a man he could trust to live the rest of his life with. That was just one more thing his experience with Emilio had taken from him.

But dwelling on that sadness wasn't going to get the job done. Kitt forced himself to concentrate on honing his blade, then smoothing those rough edges with his strop, which he managed to hang on the handle of the sliding door. The rhythmic process of both held its own soothing fascination. He got into the groove of his actions and something akin to excitement chased away any sadness or awkwardness. He was in his element, sure in his competence and eager to serve his client. The fact that Scott didn't exactly fall into that category didn't matter. Kitt wanted to please him, couldn't wait to see the man's reaction when he felt the ultra-smoothness of his skin once Kitt was done.

He removed the towel and confirmed with a light brush of his fingers that the whiskers were soft enough. Scott jerked his head almost undetectably before going limp. The aloe gel didn't lather up the way shaving cream would, but Kitt did his best with his badger brush to make it foamy. As with everything else, he'd spent the extra money to get the best brush. He hadn't been raised in wealth and quality of anything had been in short supply, but he'd been determined to spend his money on things that mattered and lasted rather than on the transient things that would make him happy for a short while before fading away.

Once Scott's face was sufficiently covered, Kitt took a bracing breath before he got down to the part that required a lot of touching. It was critical that his hands be steady. The last thing he wanted was to nick Scott. A sense of pride, if nothing else, gave him even more determination, and when he reached for the man's face, he was pleased to see how in control he was. The last test came when he had to place the fingertips of his left hand on Scott's temple area to give himself control in order to shave. There was that spark, a full-body one, that landed in his groin. He was almost used to it now, and with his purpose clear, it was easy to ignore it entirely. There was a twitch of muscle underneath his fingers, subtle yet undeniable, that indicated Scott was affected by the contact too. Kitt told himself that it was discomfort at having a blade close to his jugular. Reading anything else into the reaction would be ridiculous.

After the first touch, the rest was easy. Kitt was back in the groove, concentrating on each stroke of his blade. The rasping noise of stubble being removed blended with the rest of the natural sounds around them. It became part of the peaceful environment that chased away his fears and allowed him to revel in delight over his chosen profession. Scott remained compliant, allowing Kitt to tilt his head this way and that as he methodically cleared his cheeks, chin and throat. Kitt used his fingers as well as his eyes to scrutinize his work. When he was satisfied, he stepped back and took up the towel.

"Don't move. I'm not done yet."

So saying, he repeated his efforts at lathering Scott's face with the aloe, this time using his fingers to cover the entire area, and shaved him again. While he could have stopped after the first time, he wanted Scott to have the benefit of the best shave possible. When the second pass was done, he rinsed the wet towel in cool water and returned to clean Scott's face. By the time he was slapping witch hazel over the shorn skin, it was indeed as soft as a baby's bottom — the perfect result.

Kitt stepped back and got busy cleaning up. "You're all set. I hope you liked it." He didn't have the courage to face Scott as he spoke. It was silly, but now that he was done with his job, shyness and insecurity creeped back in.

There was a creak from the chaise and the looming shape of Scott standing filled Kitt's peripheral vision. "It's amazing, the best shave I've ever had."

Hearing those words of praise caused Kitt's chest to swell and he couldn't hold back a wide grin. Scott was stroking his chin with one hand. "I'm glad you like it."

Scott fixed his bright blue eyes on Kitt. "I've seriously never had a better one. No one has taken two passes at it before."

"That's one of the tricks," Kitt replied with sure knowledge, "especially with thick whiskers like yours." Somehow the inference of Scott's overt masculinity sent Kitt back into shyness mode. There was just no helping it, apparently. Scott's presence was destined to throw him off kilter for the remainder of his stay. "I'll just get all this put back." Kitt hurriedly turned back to his task.

"Okay, I'll meet you out at my rental car."

It took a moment for Kitt to remember that they were planning a trip to the store. "Great… I won't take long."

Not wanting to keep the man waiting, Kitt double-timed his efforts, and after slipping on his sneakers, left the house through the front door for the first time since he'd arrived. He didn't hesitate, probably because he could see Scott waiting for him by the open driver's door to his rental SUV. He didn't even bother looking around for Emilio to come jumping out at him. There was no need to. Scott was a man trained to be aware of his surroundings. He really was Kitt's bodyguard, whether either of them wanted him to be or not.

Flicking his sunglasses on, Kitt walked out into the glorious day without a scintilla of fear.

Chapter Five

Scott navigated the narrow roads of the town with practiced ease. He'd learned to drive here the summer after he'd turned sixteen. Because the height of the season was still weeks away, there weren't that many summer residents milling about. It was always easier to drive when people weren't stepping out onto the streets at random intervals — not that he was unused to that, either. He'd spent a great deal of time navigating people, as well as livestock, in countries where traffic laws were mostly suggestions. People were people the world over, he'd found, so he wasn't surprised that even in a town with strict laws about where to cross, pedestrians still ignored them.

But no, there was nothing out there that disturbed him. It was more about that one person sitting next to him that made for distracted driving — not that it was Kitt's fault. This was entirely Scott's problem, the inability to take his mind and other parts off the guy for more than two seconds. God, he was being pitiful. He kept wanting to take his hand off the wheel to feel the buttery softness of his own cheek. It wasn't merely because it felt good, but because it reminded him of the disturbing appeal of Kitt's tender touches as he'd scraped the stubble away with such a sure hand that not once had Scott worried about being nicked. No other shave he'd received had ever stolen Scott's concentration as much, nor left him with a sense of disappointment when it stopped. It already haunted him with visions of Kitt ministering to him every morning in just that way — and maybe others, as well. 'Disturbing' didn't come close to describing his errant thoughts.

Pull yourself together, Carpenter.

He concentrated on hunting down a parking space. There was a municipal lot in the town center that cost very little, but he kind of prided himself on finding convenient on-street parking. He barked out a "ha" when he spotted a space just a few feet away from his destination. He parallel parked the rental in one shot and was ridiculously pleased at doing so, especially when Kitt remarked on it.

As he released his seatbelt, the young man said, "That was impressive. I'm so terrible at parking on the street unless I can pull into it. Even then, I fret over backing out again without hitting anyone. Thank God I live in the time of back-up cameras. Frankly, I can't wait for self-driving cars to become the norm."

"Parallel parking is not that hard once you learn the trick of it. I could teach you if you'd like." The offer popped out of his mouth before he could stop it.

Fortunately, Kitt shot down the idea. "Thanks, but many have tried, and all have failed. Besides, I don't know why I'm prattling on about driving. I'm a city dweller without a car, so…" He shrugged and got out.

Scott couldn't quite manage to avert his gaze as it homed in on Kitt's tight, high ass with its painted-on jeans. Appalled at his behavior, however secretive, Scott left the vehicle and joined Kitt on the sidewalk. He led the way to the local market. It wasn't as cost-effective as the large chain store outside of town, nor did it have the same variety, but the owners were a family that his had known for years. It was comforting to go someplace small and familiar, plus it helped the local economy. Out of habit, he scanned the area for danger and made sure he was positioned in a way to grab Kitt if he needed protection. He didn't even try to temper his automatic instincts, because while he wasn't currently in a war zone, there was still the possibility of a domestic tango out there ready to pounce.

Part of him almost wanted that fucker, Emilio, to make a move so that he could mete out the justice the guy deserved. *Strike the 'almost'.* He clenched his hands at the thought of pounding Kitt's tormentor into a bloody pulp. He forced his fingers to relax, the saner part of him knowing that Kitt was better off having an excursion that didn't turn into a bloodbath and a police report. Opening the door to the Downeast Quick Mart, he ushered his houseguest inside the small store of his childhood memories. A sharp inhale sent him reeling back to those happier times. Everything not only looked the same, but it also smelled the same. The McNallys had owned the place for three generations and they still made their own baked goods in the back. The scent of fresh sub rolls made him want to head straight for the deli section and order his favorite Italian sub, loaded. He had no idea what the family did to make those the best he'd ever tasted, but it was still true.

"Um, shall we get one cart or two?"

Kitt's timid question caught Scott's attention. The guy was standing with obvious uncertainty, holding on to the handle of one of the small shopping carts. It took a moment for Scott to understand what he was really asking.

Pulling the cart gently from Kitt's grasp, he said, "One. It will hold enough to last us a few days. We can always come back for more whenever we need it." He leaned in a little closer, momentarily as intoxicated by the scent of Kitt as he had been with the baked goods. "This is household related. That means it's my treat. You get that, right?"

Kitt visibly relaxed but he also gnawed briefly at his lower lip before replying. "Yeah, and thanks. I don't really have any money, but I'm going to pay you and Karen back once I get a new job. I swear."

Because he could see that this was important to Kitt, Scott didn't dismiss the vow. "I have no doubt about that," he said, even though he was never going to accept any money from the guy and knew that Karen wouldn't, either. But he understood how a man needed his pride. He stood staring into the man's eyes to convey…he wasn't sure what. He just liked doing it. Kitt didn't seem to mind. If anything, his attention was equally fixated on Scott.

"Scott Carpenter, as I live and breathe."

They were forced to break their gaze as the current proprietor of the market came down to their end of the counter. Scott grinned. "Mrs. McNally, how are you, ma'am?"

The woman, who was a little older than his mother had been, primped the iron-gray bun on the back of her head. "Well, the arthritis is acting up, what with the wet spring we've had, but you know me, mustn't grumble."

He did know her, and grumbling was kind of her thing, but when major storms threatened the town or displaced people, she was the first to arrive with helping hands and supplies and the last to leave after the disaster passed. She was the kind of woman who communities all over the world depended on. Just seeing her standing in her worn apron with a dusting of flour on her cheek, sent a wave of nostalgia and almost sadness coursing through him. He was mortified to feel tears starting to form at the corner of his eyes.

Kitt bumped him over a few inches with his hip, taking the woman's attention. "Hi, Mrs. McNally. We haven't been introduced, but I'm Kitt, a friend of Karen's. We were in a few days ago."

"I sure do remember, sweetie. Looks like you've got yourself a roommate now, huh?"

Kitt chuffed out a laugh. "Yes, ma'am. Karen and Scott got their wires a little crossed, so of course, the food we bought is running out. I swear, I've never seen anyone eat as much as Scott does in one sitting."

Mrs. McNally laughed, too, and rolled her eyes. "All of those muscles need fuel. I always knew Scott would do something exciting with his life, but a Navy SEAL?" She fanned the end of her apron as if the oven had just exploded in a ball of heat.

Embarrassed by how he was now being discussed as if he were some hot piece of ass, Scott lost all sense of melancholy. "Well, if you will excuse my manly muscles and me, we're going to head for the red-meat section." He flashed a smile to show he wasn't offended.

"Good idea." Kitt joined him by his side and looked up at him for a second. There was something in his expression that revealed to Scott that the boy had understood Scott's emotional reaction and had deliberately deflected Mrs. McNally to help Scott get himself under control. Scott couldn't even articulate why that was so obvious to him with that quick glance, but it was. He was grateful for it, especially given that Kitt had revealed his name, making things riskier for himself than they needed to be — not that the people in town couldn't be trusted. It was simply that the more people who knew where Kitt was, the more likely it was that Emilio could find him.

As they sauntered down the first aisle, Scott murmured, "Thanks. You didn't have to do that."

"Do what?" Kitt picked up a bag of green grapes and dangled it in front of Scott with an unspoken question.

Okay, so apparently they weren't going to acknowledge what had just happened, and that was fine with Scott. He was embarrassed enough on a few fronts already. When he nodded, Kitt dropped the bag into the cart.

They continued in that vein, aisle after aisle. It was reminiscent of the many times he'd been in the store with his mother, Grammy or Karen — very domestic, which should have freaked him out, yet somehow didn't. The only problem was that he had to keep a keen eye on Kitt. The guy was clearly reluctant to pick out things that he wanted, couching all suggestions as to what Scott desired. That wouldn't do. Kitt was his guest and it was important to Scott that he enjoy his stay. Food was an important part of the social fabric of everyone's lives. He'd learned that lesson on his deployments as well as at home. Bonds were formed over meals and food could also be used as a weapon to control people. He'd bet Emilio, the fucker, had done that with Kitt, so Scott was determined to give the boy anything he wanted in that market. It took some coaxing and patience, but eventually, Kitt started putting things into the cart without asking Scott first.

When they circled back to the front counter, Scott gave in to the desire that had been nagging him since walking through the door. "We have to get subs for lunch," he said, practically pressing his nose to the glass covering the meat selection as he'd done as a kid.

Kitt joined him. "Sure, whatever you want, but I don't mind cooking something."

"I'll take you up on that offer tonight for dinner, but I'm practically drooling at the prospect of having one of McNally's Italian subs."

Mrs. McNally joined them, chuckling as she approached. "Only one? Who are you trying to fool, Scotty?"

"Not you, ma'am, that's for sure. I'll take four, if you please. Even if I don't eat them all today, they taste even better after an overnight stay in the refrigerator. I'm sure you remember how I like them."

"I do, indeed and have gotten a jump on your predictable order. What would you like...Kitt, was it?"

Kitt fidgeted. "I'm not sure. I guess I'll have one of whatever Scott is ordering."

Mrs. McNally looked down her nose at him. "Are you sure? He likes his with extra hot peppers."

"Oh." Kitt gnawed at his lower lip again, an obvious sign that he was agitated. Just as Scott was about to step in, the boy visibly straightened and said, "I'm actually not a big fan of hot anything."

Mrs. McNally nodded. "No hot peppers, then. How about onions? They're raw."

"That's fine, thanks." He glanced at Scott as if looking for reassurance. Scott was happy to oblige with a quick nod of his own.

"Oh my God, Scott, is that you?"

They both turned toward a pretty blonde woman who approached with a basket over her arm and wearing a T-shirt and jeans that accentuated her generous curves. Scott recognized that he knew her yet couldn't come up with a name. The woman stopped next to Kitt, staring over his head as if he didn't exist, and smiled brightly at Scott.

"You don't remember me."

"Um."

"It's fine, really. I was like five years younger than you when we summered up here at the same time. I guess I still am," she added with a flirtatious giggle. "Your sister would babysit me sometimes at your place, and I would follow you around like a puppy dog."

The penny dropped—in the almost literal sense. "Penny Young."

"That's right."

"How are you?"

"Great." Her gaze raked him from head to toe. "I'd heard you were in the military or something."

"Yeah, the Navy." He didn't bother with the whole SEAL thing. Sometimes it started the conversation down the wrong path, like, *Really… Can you kill people with your bare hands?* And that question was typically followed up with, *"How many have you killed?"* While he had always ignored those types of questions, he did sometimes capitalize on women's fascination with his profession for the purpose of getting laid. He didn't like that about himself after the fact, but he'd still done it. This wasn't one of those times, however.

"That's so interesting," Penny gushed. "I'm just waiting tables at the Crab Shack these days. My history degree hasn't proven as useful as I thought. I'm trying to figure out my next move."

Scott shifted his feet, uncomfortable at how Kitt was being left out of the conversation, while also not wanting to bring him into it. Nobody further needed to know his identity. And yet, he felt as if Kitt was a natural part of his orbit now and pretending he didn't exist was disconcerting. Best to end the conversation as quickly as possible.

"Yeah, I was lucky to find my passion so early. Lots of people need more time to figure out what they want to do professionally."

Penny cocked a hip, signaling that she wasn't leaving any time soon. "Well, the money's good anyway, especially when the season gets into full swing."

"Here you go." Mrs. McNally slapped the subs on the counter. She was lightning-fast when it came to filling orders. "Why don't you finish your shopping while I ring Penny up? Come on, girl. Don't keep me waiting."

Clearly affronted at the intervention, Penny slow-walked her way backward to the register, her gaze still on Scott. "Come by for dinner sometime — at the Shack, I mean. It's good to see you." She turned then, and Scott could swear there was a swing to her hips that could not be natural.

"Jesus," he muttered, running a hand down his face before he grabbed the subs.

"She seems nice." This from Kitt, who was yes, again, running his teeth over that lower lip. It was a wonder it wasn't bleeding from all that attention.

"Like she said, she's just some bratty kid that Karen used to babysit. Drove me crazy."

"Yeah, but she's not a little girl anymore."

"Something she's making sure I noticed. Forget her. What else do you want?"

Kitt glanced around before shrugging. "Nothing. We've hit all the aisles."

"Good. Me too. Let's check out and go home."

He deliberately dawdled, though, so that Penny was gone by the time he stepped up to the cash register. It wasn't until he was done loading the SUV and heading for the driver's seat door that he realized how he'd referred to the cottage. *Home.* It was his for sure, but it seemed fitting to express it as such for Kitt, too. Scott didn't give it more than a glancing thought, however, because it felt right.

Kitt feels right, and that *is the disturbing part.*

He lowered the windows on the drive back, enjoying breathing the sea air, the feel of it on his smooth cheeks. That thought led his mind back to his companion. Kitt was resting his head against the seat, his eyes closed, his face turned toward the open window. The hint of a smile confirmed that he found the ride pleasing. He was almost puppy-like in his open joy. Neither of them said anything, and Scott was tempted to take a long, circuitous route simply to extend the pleasant outing. But the groceries included ice cream and other foods that didn't fare well, even in an air-conditioned vehicle, so he stayed the impulse. All too soon, they pulled up to the house.

Once again, Scott did a quick visual scan of the area to make sure no one was lurking.

Hopping out, he continued his scan on the way to the back of his SUV. Then he grabbed a lighter bag and handed it to Kitt when he joined him. "Here... I'll walk you in and return for the rest."

"You don't have to. I have keys." Kitt reached for his pocket.

"No." Scott spoke firmly but not to frighten him. He put his hand on Kitt's arm to stop him. The warmth of the skin reminded him of the boy's burn, but more, it reminded him of how disconcerting he was.

Scott pulled his hand away instantly. "I want to clear the house. I mean, I want to check and make sure it hasn't been broken into," he amended when Kitt blinked at him in confusion. "Not that there's any likelihood of that," he added quickly because he could see the fear seeping into Kitt's eyes. "It's my training. That's all. Hard to turn it off."

With that half-truth uttered, he did as promised, making sure that the first floor and the second were both empty and that there was no sign of a break-in. When he trotted back down, he found Kitt in the kitchen already putting the groceries away. "All clear. I'll bring the rest of the bags in."

Scott raced back out before Kitt could argue about the distribution of tasks. It made sense, anyway. It only took two trips to empty the SUV. They spent a few minutes working side-by-side to store it all away before Scott felt the smallness of the area pressing in on him. In fact, it felt as if the entire house were shrinking, which was moronic. This was his own mental health problem — or perhaps it was more accurate to say the issue was somewhere south. His attraction to Kitt was growing, not shrinking. *And you don't want this, remember?*

"I need a run," he blurted out.

Kitt nodded. "Okay. I'll get started on the potato salad. That way, it will be chilled enough by dinner time. We can have that with the burgers."

"Great." Scott was already on the way to the stairs. "I'll fire up the grill later and we can cook them outside."

"Oh, that's a wonderful idea. I haven't done a cook-out in, like…forever."

Kitt's obvious delight made Scott feel like Alice in Wonderland — growing ten feet tall while the house shrank around him. He really needed to get outside and work off some of this…whatever was going on with him.

He only needed to change into running shorts and shoes. For this run, he wanted speed more than strength-building. He headed out through the deck to hit the beach, making a point of not looking in the direction of the kitchen, although he could hear Kitt moving around in there and the faint whirl of the exhaust fan. The day was perfect for a nice jog. But the antsy feeling under his skin caused him to pick up speed as soon as his muscles loosened. He knew from long experience that he could go half a mile before running into an outcropping of rock. It was an easy stretch to traverse for someone like him, hardly a workout at all. So, he looped around and ran to the house, pouring on the speed, only to do the same again when he was within a few feet of the deck.

Four and a half miles into his run, sweat poured down his face and his clothing stuck to his skin. It wasn't enough, though. Without any distractions, his mind raced faster than his feet, with visions of his last deployment and the fatal attack flashing across his brain like a kaleidoscope. Worse, in some ways, was that visions of Kitt started to intersperse with the other memories, as if his subconscious were trying to insert the boy into the past horrors of Scott's life. No amount of physical exertion was helping, so he stopped abruptly, stripped down to just his shorts and plunged into the Atlantic.

The frigid water took his breath away. He was used to swimming in all kinds of temperatures, but always with the proper gear. The human body was no match for the cold water off the shore of New England. As a kid, he'd swum and boogie-boarded until his lips had turned blue and his teeth chattered — or until his mother or Grammy had scolded him back onto shore. As an adult, he'd known better than to court hypothermia, but not on this day. He swam against the current in the hope that cold would do for him what the heat had not. By the time he dragged himself onto the beach near his pile of clothing, he was limp with exhaustion. The fine grain of the sand pricked at his skin as it dried, while the salt water made it stiff. And yet, as he lay under the bruising rays of the sun, irritated by the natural assaults on his flesh, his mind was still cluttered and busy.

With a groan, he rolled onto his stomach, then up onto his knees and finally his feet. There was no point in remaining uncomfortable when it served no good purpose. At least his dick had shriveled, and his balls were hugging his body as close as possible. He didn't have to worry about throwing any wood in Kitt's face when he returned to the cottage. Grabbing his shirt and sneakers, he started walking. The return trek was pleasant, though, as he splashed his feet in the cool shallow water. The sand mostly sloughed off his skin with every step. The gulls circled him, per usual, so he forced himself to focus on them and the sight and sound of the waves crashing. It reminded him of how he was such a small part of something huge and beautiful. Allowing himself to be swallowed up by his relatively insignificant problems wasn't going to do him any good. Bad things happened and still the wondrous world kept going, bringing the promise of new hope each day.

When he approached the deck, however, the truth of his observation was there for him to see. His gaze homed in on it—on *him*—whether he wanted it to or not. There was Kitt, waiting for him on one of the chairs, the table set for lunch. After all that he'd been through, this young man had the courage and resilience to pick up the pieces of his life and start again. Knowing that made Scott embarrassed about dwelling so obsessively on his own problems. Kitt was such a welcoming sight that Scott recognized the sting of moisture in his eyes. He told himself it was the sun and the salt from the ocean, but he knew better. And that self-awareness bothered him enough that he was selfishly brisk with his houseguest as he shouted up to him.

"I need to shower off. No point in waiting for me."

He avoided seeing how Kitt took the announcement, instead heading for the outside shower. He let the tepid water sluice down his body with his shorts still on. As he'd forgotten to bring a towel out with him, he had to put his T-shirt and sneakers on with wet skin. No, he *chose* to do so. There was something about the idea of sitting bare chested next to Kitt that made him feel awkward. Shy, even. He preferred to deal with cloth sticking to him instead of those messy emotions.

As he trudged up the stairs, he saw that Kitt hadn't started eating. Rather, he sat under the shadow of the deck's awning, watching him. His expression was unreadable, pleasant, but perhaps a little wary, which bothered Scott and added to his feelings of guilt. He forced a smile in order to ease any concerns and was rewarded when Kitt returned the expression.

"Did you have a good run?" Kitt asked the question while he poured them both a glass of iced tea and waved a fly away from Scott's plate of food.

Scott dropped heavily in his chair and chugged most of the glass before answering. "Yeah." He filled his glass again, relishing the cool, wet surface of the pitcher.

"I don't know how you can do it for so long in this heat. I'm a gym rat, myself. Give me air-conditioning when I work up a sweat." The boy raised half his sub and took a delicate bite.

Scott fisted his as well and brought it close to his mouth. "I have to be able to block out the temperature. There's no climate control out where I spend most of my tours." He opened his mouth to take a big chunk of his sandwich and froze as Kitt's face morphed into a picture of orgasmic-level pleasure.

"Oh my God, that's so good!" Kitt exclaimed, even as he chewed his food.

Scott grinned like an idiot. "I know, right? It's like the McNally family has some kind of secret spice they add." So saying, he tore a huge hunk of sub off with his teeth, filling his mouth with the taste of everything that was good from his childhood memories.

"Mm-m. Mm-m." Kitt's moans coupled with flashing hazel eyes caused Scott's mouthful to get temporarily caught in his throat.

He reached for his glass and chugged down more tea. His dick also tried to rally from its cold-induced slumber. He punched it surreptitiously to stop that nonsense fast, while he took another bite. Concentrating on his food and drink was hard to do but ultimately safer and saner. Fortunately, Kitt's appreciation for his meal dimmed into something far less distracting. They ate in companionable silence that was interrupted just by the gulls and the waves and the buzzing of insects. It took only a few minutes for Scott to relax and just let it all be. It was perhaps the most pleasant half hour or so he'd ever spent in his life. The horror of his memories and the distraction that was Kitt seemed to meet somewhere in the middle so that he just felt *good*.

With the last of his second sub filling his stomach, Scott sat back with a sigh. His eyelids drooped with sudden fatigue. "Wow, I'm like a baby after glutting myself with a bottle. I feel like a nap, which isn't like me at all." He punctuated the observation with a huge yawn. When his eyes were fully open again, he saw Kitt smiling.

"You're on vacation. Naps are practically obligatory. Go ahead," he added, standing and reaching for Scott's plate.

"No, I've got that." Once again, with stupidity being the watchword of the day, Scott put his hand on Kitt's, trying to stop him.

This time, however, instead of snatching it back from the spark that the contact produced, Scott perversely left it there. The warmth and softness of

Kitt's skin was intoxicating. Before he could stop himself, Scott ran his thumb along the silky smoothness and over the delicate wrist bone within his grasp. A sharp inhalation of breath caused him to look into Kitt's eyes, where he found that wariness again. If that had been all, Scott would have let go immediately, but there was more. Intrigue, perhaps. His pupils were definitely larger, obscuring the beauty of the brown-green irises. Kitt's lips were parted ever so slightly, and as they stared at one another, the boy swept his tongue across them.

A strange and almost overwhelming urge to lunge across the table and capture that mouth with his own bolted through Scott. The shock of it brought him to his senses. Letting go of Kitt, he tried to take the plate instead. "You served. I'll clear."

Kitt tugged it away with surprising strength. "Don't be ridiculous. I just put stuff out." Was that hurt in his tone? "If you want, you can wash up after dinner, although you'll be doing most of the cooking as I can't grill worth a damn." With hasty movements, he picked up everything from the table, impressively juggling it all. "I guess I have trouble assessing the heat or something. Anyway, I've made the potato salad and I'm going to make brownies for sundaes after dinner, so maybe we can share the clean-up duties." With what definitely sounded like a huff, he turned to the sliding doors, then stood there when it was obvious that he couldn't open them with his hands full.

Scott solved that problem in a flash, opening the doors without getting too close to his houseguest. "Here." He swept his hand in a moronically formal gesture for Kitt to pass.

"Thank you," Kitt said primly, and this time, his tone was not open to misinterpretation. He took one step inside before stopping. "Honestly, Scott, this is your house and your vacation. Do whatever you want, but please allow me to feel at least useful...and not intrusive. Or disturbing." He flashed a vulnerable look that made Scott feel like shit, even as he couldn't quite figure out what he had done to create, or should do to correct, the problem.

"I want you to feel like a guest and not like you have to wait on me or something." That was not the whole of what Kitt was saying or how Scott was feeling, but it was the safer topic.

Kitt looked at him from over his shoulder. "That's not what I am, though. I'm a problem. Trouble, even," he added, lowering his gaze.

"Hey?" He waited until Kitt was looking at him again before continuing. "I'm a SEAL. We look for trouble and love solving problems—neither of which you are, by the way. I'm just saying," he added with a shrug.

Kitt pursed his lips. "Fine. Whatever." Obviously not convinced, Kitt flounced over to the kitchen.

Scott found himself watching the show all the way until Kitt's cute rear end was hidden by the counter. With an internal shake, he entered the house and closed the sliding doors. *What the fuck is my problem?* There really was no accounting for his vacillating and conflicting thoughts, urges, feelings... They were crazy and confusing. Kitt didn't need to be on the receiving end of Scott's inner rollercoaster. So, he plopped onto the couch and clicked through the channels until he found two teams playing baseball. It didn't even matter which ones he was watching. He just needed the distraction, and when his eyelids started to droop, he didn't fight it.

Chapter Six

"Scott? Scott? Wakey, wakey."

His eyes were wide open before the last syllable was uttered. He sat upright on the couch, assessing his situation in the split second the movement took. Kitt was wisely a few feet away, somehow knowing to keep his distance when waking him. *Or no, probably because he learned that maneuver the hard way with his fucker of an ex-boyfriend. No matter.* Scott was glad that he hadn't been in a position to startle the boy any more than necessary.

He yawned and rubbed the sleep from his eyes. "What time is it?"

"Almost six. I figured you'd want to start the grill."

Yawning again, Scott stood and stretched. "Yeah, you're right."

Kitt headed for the kitchen. "Great. I have some marinated peppers and onions on skewers to go along with the burgers and potato salad. I hope you don't mind grilling them."

"No, that's a good idea. I'll hit the head then get started."

In the downstairs half-bath, he eyed himself in the mirror. God, he looked a mess, and why it mattered was something he didn't want to explore. It was exhausting trying to keep up with his shifting thoughts and feelings at the moment. Still, he splashed water on his face and head to rearrange himself into something more presentable before leaving the bathroom.

Kitt was already out on the deck, staring at the giant grill. When Scott joined him, he said, "This is a serious piece of equipment."

Scott grinned. "I remember the day I went shopping with my father for this baby. He'd been using an old charcoal one that my grandparents had. My grandpa had insisted that food didn't taste as good when cooked with gas. But the summer after he died, Grammy gave the okay to switch over. My old man spent hours researching for just the right one." He ran his hand along the steel trim. "That first night, we had hotdogs and burgers and, as I've always recalled, they tasted fantastic, probably because I'd been involved in the purchase. My dad even let me flip a few patties."

His breath stuttered out with the intensity of the memory. Then he made the mistake of looking at Kitt.

The boy's eyes were moist. "That's lovely. You must miss him in particular at a time like this."

Scott swallowed down the lump clogging his throat. "Yeah. He was a good man. He taught me how to be the same." And, because the emotions were once more getting too strong, he looked away and lightened up. "Let's get going. I'm starving."

Kitt, bless him, took the hint. He helped Scott load the grill with the food, brought him an ice-cold beer without him needing to ask, then stood aside in companionable silence and let him do his thing.

The night was perfect, and the meal was delicious, even if he did say so himself. A second bottle of beer helped him relax, as did the ease with which Kitt made small talk, while never getting too close or too heavy with topics. They feasted on the deck, then Scott cleaned up. Kitt didn't try to dissuade him, but he did make massive brownie sundaes for them both. They ate them while watching TV before heading to bed.

It was all perfectly pleasant — until the nightmare came.

* * * *

At first, Kitt thought his own voice had woken him. God knew the wounded animal sound was familiar. But, no… As he sat forward in bed, arms hugging his waist, he knew that couldn't be true. The noise was still audible, and while his heart pounded with worry, there was no lingering, sweaty fear from a nightmare plaguing him. The moaning and garbled words were coming from outside the bedroom, and that could only mean one thing.

"Scott…" Kitt was out of bed and heading into the hallway before he considered the risk he was taking approaching a powerful man in distress. All he could think about was that the man he was living with, the one he'd shared a lovely dinner with, was suffering.

"No! Fuck, no! Come on, J.J. Stay with me, man."

The obvious pain lacing each growled word stabbed at Kitt's heart as he crept down the hall toward Scott's door. He paused there, his ear pressed against the wood, heartbeat hammering with growing apprehension. He wanted to go in to help Scott weather his nightmare. Still, he hesitated, in fear of how his well-intentioned intervention might be met.

It was the heart-rending sob that made his decision for him. No matter the consequences to himself, he had to try to help. The man had been so kind to him and he was *not* Emilio. If Scott ended up lashing out, it would be because he wasn't fully awake and aware of what was happening. Only a coward or callous person would leave Scott on his own during a time like this. Even after all he'd been through, Kitt hoped he hadn't turned into either of those things.

Squaring his shoulders, he slowly opened the door and peeked inside. "Scott?"

Through the sliver of moonlight coming past the shades, he was easy to spot. Scott sat curled over his raised knees, staring straight ahead. "Where's Hassan?" The timber of his voice had dropped even lower, the pain underlying it somehow rawer.

Kitt stepped into the room. "Scott? You're having a nightmare. It's okay to wake up. You're safe," he added, although it seemed strange for him to say something like that. He was hardly in a position to protect anyone, and yet, in that moment, he felt fiercely capable.

A second ticked by, then another, before Scott showed any sign that he'd heard and knew he was no longer alone. Slowly, he turned his head to face Kitt. Even in the dimness and with half the room between them, the utter devastation in his eyes was clear to see. "It's gone," he croaked. "His beautiful face is gone." He convulsed on another sob.

Kitt had no hesitation now. He raced to the bed and slid onto it to reach out and wrap his arms around

Scott's massive chest. There was such elemental power to the SEAL, physical strength for which Kitt would have no defense. But at that moment, all that mattered was his emotional vulnerability and the fact that Kitt had the ability to offer him what he needed—a safety net to vent his feelings and a source from which to draw comfort.

Scott stayed stiff and unmoving for longs seconds, leaving Kitt to wonder if he was still in the throes of the nightmare and not awake. Then that big body suddenly twisted to sag against him. He curled into Kitt's embrace, laying his cheek against his shoulder. Scott's hot breath bathed the skin of Kitt's neck as he shuddered and hugged Kitt almost too tight. He wasn't quite crying—or if he was, it was the kind of dry, heaving process that Kitt associated with overly masculine men.

Ignoring a part of him that warned to keep some distance between himself and this potentially lethal man, he closed the minor gap between their bodies and pressed into him. The reassuring warmth of Scott seeped past their layers of clothing, leaving Kitt momentarily confused about who was comforting whom. But the sweat mingled with the noticeable tremors served as a reminder.

Kitt rubbed Scott's back with slow circles. "It's okay. You're safe and you are not alone. I have you."

It felt as if those words, as inadequate as they seemed, did the trick. Scott relaxed more and his breath evened out. He roamed the small of Kitt's back with his fingers, sending little shocks skittering up his spine. Scott's mouth replaced his breath in tickling the side of Kitt's neck. He froze as those lips slid the length of his throat, covering each inch, until they pressed against his jaw and lingered there. Kitt held his breath, not sure what to do, how to respond. Was Scott still dreaming? Did he think he was hugging some former or current girlfriend? No, he'd know if Scott was involved with someone. The man would have said something, surely. Or maybe he thought Kitt was Hassan—Hassan with the beautiful face, who had obviously met a tragic fate. Except that made no sense.

Scott is straight. Isn't he?

There was no time to answer his own question. In the blink of an eye, Scott went from nuzzling to full-on kissing. He captured Kitt's mouth with an intensity that bordered on painful. But before he could object, Scott gentled his assault. It was no less passionate, yet somehow softened, their lips melding. When the man's tongue begged entrance, Kitt hesitated only a moment before letting him in. He waited tensely for feelings of being overwhelmed and fearful, but they didn't come. There was something about Scott that simply didn't engender those responses. It gave Kitt renewed hope. He fisted Scott's T-shirt and joined the fray with a nascent passion. He kissed him back with increasing need that led Kitt to whimper—with delight, not distress.

And an instant later, everything changed. Scott first froze, his tongue still locked around Kitt's, then bolted from the embrace with such force and speed that it nearly sent Kitt tumbling to the floor. Kitt crouched on the bed, his fingers fisted around the sheet instead of Scott's rock-hard body. The man who had only a moment ago embraced him with obvious desire now stood on the opposite side of the bed, his eyes wild as he stared back. Scott opened his mouth a couple of times before any words came out.

"I'm sorry." Scott huffed as if he'd just run some of those beach suicides that he loved so much. Then he held out his hands as if to grab Kitt. "Are you all right? I didn't hurt you, did I?"

Well, that was an interesting question and one that didn't have an easy answer. He knew, of course, that Scott was worried about how hard he'd shoved Kitt away the second he'd realized that he was kissing a dude. And naturally, the answer to that was that Kitt was fine. He hadn't landed with his ass hitting the floor. Although even if he had, that would have been nothing compared to the strange ache blooming in the middle of his chest. He wanted to rub at it yet resisted.

With as much pride as he could muster, he slid off the bed and stood straight, looking at Scott. "I'm fine." He tugged at his T-shirt in a useless effort to hide the fact that his dick was filling his bikini briefs. He was happy to know that his libido seemed to have returned at full strength, while also unwilling to expose too much of his feelings in front of someone who had soundly rejected him.

Scott's gaze flicked down with Kitt's movement, which would have been completely mortifying if not for the fact that the man didn't appear to be aware that his own cock was practically bursting through his boxers. A visible shudder ran through him and he ran his hand through his hair. "I'm, ah, sorry. I was still caught up in my dream and didn't know what I was doing." He stared rather warily at Kitt.

You mean nightmare, one in which—Jesus—*someone's face had been blown off or something.* Kitt grimaced. Scott's words were not surprising. They were right up there with the age-old excuse of having been so drunk that some closeted guy had missed that the mouth blowing him the night before belonged to another man. *Yeah, right.* Disappointment washed over him, threatening to drown him in the depressing predictability of it all. But what did he expect? Scott was the epitome of the alpha male, and whether he was suppressing the fact that he was gay or perhaps bisexual, it didn't matter. The last thing Kitt needed was more drama in his life. And shame on him for thinking for one second that Scott could be more than a reluctant roommate.

Pride made him straighten even more and blink back tears that threatened to leak out. "You don't have to explain yourself to me." He was glad that his voice didn't waver. "I only came in because you were having a bad dream and sounded upset. I wanted to make sure you were all right. And you are, so..." He shrugged.

Scott ran the back of his hand across his mouth. Kitt tried not to think that he was wiping away the remnants of the kiss. "I'm sorry," Scott said again, "that I woke you."

Kitt waved away the apology. "No worries. It's not like I have to get up early or anything."

"Still...it won't happen again. I'm fine. It was nothing, really."

Kitt turned to leave, then stopped at the doorway and looked over his shoulder. "You know, I'm not like a therapist or anything...obviously. But it seems to me that what you do is stressful and horrific on a level that I can't even imagine. And I admire that you can do that stuff to keep us all safe and everything, but...dude, for what it's worth, I don't think you're *fine*. Not being fine is kind of something I'm an expert at. What I've learned in these last few days of my life is that asking for help to make things better for you is okay."

He didn't wait for Scott to respond. Instead, he returned to his own bed, curled onto his side and lay there waiting for sleep to return, trying to forget the feeling of Scott's lips on his own.

* * * *

When the first hint of daylight showed through the edges of the curtains, Kitt finally gave up trying to get back to sleep. He rose and went down to the kitchen to make himself some coffee. Then he sat out on the deck and watched the sun rise with all its beauty and natural signs of hope. It was a new day, so anything was possible. He chose to expect positive things and decidedly rejected brooding over what had happened a few hours before in Scott's bedroom. No man was worth the time, energy and heartache that came from wanting what a person couldn't have. That had actually been the first lesson he'd learned as a gay boy — that far fewer people who he wanted would want him back. It had been rather crushing to accept that, although nothing compared to the lesson Emilio had meted out. When someone wanted him back on unacceptable terms, it was time to leave. Never finding a man to grow old with was better than living in constant fear from the person who supposedly loved him.

So Scott was in denial about his sexuality or he wasn't, but he chose not to act on it because he believed being straight would make his life more bearable? *Big deal. His loss.* He was still a decent man who had been kind and generous to Kitt. And how did Kitt think last night might have ended better? Maybe Scott could have stayed in that semi-fugue state long enough to actually fuck him. *Then what?* How much worse would it be to wake up next to the man and see a look of abject horror on his face? *Yeah, no.* Kitt counted himself lucky that it had ended as quickly as it had. *No harm done. No hard feelings. The end.*

He intended to move on from the matter and that was why he was surprised at himself when he went into the kitchen and started making as much noise as he damn well pleased. Being hungry, he made pancakes. Not being nasty, he made plenty of batter for a large stack for Scott, as well. When the man didn't materialize for breakfast, Kitt put the bowl into the refrigerator in case the guy wanted to make some for himself later on. Then it was on to baking muffins, and cookies—and shortcake, because he'd bought strawberries the day before. The costly, plump fruit had caught his eye, and Scott, being a generous man, had insisted on buying a quart. It would make for a nice dessert for lunch or dinner.

Then came the cleaning—the dishes, the counter and floor. He got out the vacuum cleaner, and after only a moment's hesitation, ran it. He told himself it wasn't passive-aggressive pique but being a good guest. The cottage needed constant cleaning, given the sand that invariably got inside. It wasn't that much noise, and because Scott was a Navy SEAL, he could probably sleep through the sound of bombs dropping if need be. Kitt became so engrossed in his work that he jumped when, turning around, Scott was leaning against the kitchen counter, a mug in his hand, his gaze homing in on Kitt.

"Oh!" Kitt switched the vacuum off and tossed his hair. "Sorry... Did I wake you?" He winced inwardly at his petulant tone. Being bitchy really wasn't like him.

Scott shook his head slowly. "No." He reached across the counter. "Is it okay if I have one of these muffins?"

"Sure. They're for whenever." He licked his lips, trying not to squirm under Scott's mild stare or focus on the way the man's lips wrapped around the pastry. "I'm going to make strawberry shortcake later, so don't touch the cakes."

Scott nodded. "Okay."

Kitt went to unplug the vacuum to give himself something else to look at. "There's pancake batter in the fridge if you want to make some. Or, I'm happy to make them for you." He nearly smacked his forehead with that offer. *Why am I such a suck-up?* No, being nice and kind was not something he should upbraid himself about.

It didn't matter, anyway. Scott was already shaking his head again. "You don't have to do that, thanks. I may make some later, after my run." So saying, he polished off the muffin and the mug of coffee. "Are you okay?" Scott asked the question with his back to Kitt, while putting his mug in the sink. Then he turned and looked braced for battle.

There was something in the question and Scott's demeanor that made Kitt bristle. "Of course I am. Why wouldn't I be?" When Scott merely raised his eyebrows, Kitt huffed. "Oh, get over yourself. It was only a kiss. It's not like you ravished me or anything."

Scott's gaze hardened. "I would never hurt you."

And yet, somehow, you have. Stupid! Me, not him. Kitt retracted the cord and tugged the vacuum back into the closet before responding. "You didn't," he said with more bite than he'd intended. "I'm fine, Scott. Really.

Go, run yourself into the sand, and forget about last night. It meant nothing."

He didn't wait for a reply. Instead, he raced up the stairs to change into a clean T-shirt and jeans, brush his teeth and slap on sunscreen. He wasn't going to spend the day scrubbing his ridiculous sadness away. Some time on the beach was what he needed. The sun and salt air would do him good. Before leaving the house, however, he gathered a load of laundry and got it started. He considered for a half-second doing only his own. That, however, would have been both petty and wasteful. It cost him only a few seconds and a brief, difficult memory, to enter Scott's room and grab the man's dirty clothing. By the way the bed covers were twisted, he could tell that he wasn't the only one whose night had ended with poor sleep.

"I should hope so," he muttered as he left the room.

A quick glance told him that Scott was already far down the beach. Slipping on his grungy sneakers, Kitt headed in the opposite direction. The tide was on the way out, so it was safe enough to scamper over the big rocks. Every so often, he would squat down and peer at the pools of seawater left behind. There was so much to see—barnacles, small crabs, periwinkles. He picked some up from time-to-time to stare and study before putting them back. He'd never had this chance as a child, and it was fun to play by the ocean. There was no real work for him to do and it was better than sitting glued to the TV.

After a while, he returned to the beach to walk along the wet sand left by the receding water. Scott was still a dot in the distance, although Kitt was certain that because he'd spent so long on the rocks, the SEAL had made the return trip, probably a few times. It was silly, really, to even worry about it. The beach was big enough for the two of them, and it wasn't as if they were fighting or anything. Any awkwardness was based on Kitt allowing Scott to feel guilty when there was nothing to what had happened the night before. He resolved to put it behind him and let Scott off the hook.

There were shells to pick up, and Kitt kept a few of the prettier ones. There was also a piece of green sea glass. He kept that, too. It might be evidence of some bottle being tossed where it didn't belong, but somehow the buffeting of the salt water made the trash pretty. Pinpricks of water in the sand squirted occasionally, and Kitt understood that meant clams lay below. He knew better than to try to dig them up, given that a permit was required. Seeing it did give him a sudden taste for steamers, although he didn't like asking Scott to treat him to an expensive dinner. All this money being spent on him was disturbing. He was not by nature a mooch, and while circumstances had forced his hand, there was no need for him to get greedy.

Something white caught his eye. "Ooh." He crouched down and picked up the sand dollar. "I don't have one of you yet."

"Karen loved collecting those as a child."

Scott's sudden appearance startled Kitt and he landed on his ass. The wet from the sand seeped through his pants immediately. Ignoring it, he glared at Scott. "How do you manage to sneak up on me like that?"

Scott crouched beside him, worry in his expression. "Are you okay?"

"Of course," Kitt retorted. "The three inches my butt fell didn't do any harm." Scott's bare feet caught his attention. "I suppose that's how you were so quiet."

The man had nicely formed toes. Kitt couldn't help stare at them, like he'd suddenly developed a fetish. "Doesn't it hurt?"

"Not on the sand that sits below the water mark." Scott looked over Kitt's head at the ocean and stayed silent for so long that Kitt began to worry about what was going on in the man's head. "We need to talk about what happened."

Kitt started to rise. "No, we don't." God, the last thing he wanted was to hear about was how Scott had been in the throes of his dream and had mistaken Kitt for a woman, even though he'd been clearly having a nightmare about a man.

Scott gently held Kitt down by pressing on his shoulder, then joined him by plopping his own backside onto the wet sand. "Yes, we do."

Kitt sighed. "Why? I get it. You're a straight guy who was having a really bad nightmare, whether you want to admit it or not. I was there, a convenient pair of lips to latch on to for comfort before you realized what you were doing." *Blah, blah, blah.* The quickest way to end this discussion was to pretend to buy into Scott's vision of himself.

The man nodded, although he didn't look at Kitt when he said, "You're right. I was having a fucking awful nightmare about my last deployment."

"It wasn't my fault that you ended up kissing me." Kitt felt as if he had to be on the defensive. He'd been through this too many times with Emilio, when the man regretted his actions and tried to make out like it was all Kitt's doing.

Scott looked at him with surprise. "Of course it's not. I'm not trying to blame you for what I did."

Because his declaration sounded genuine, Kitt dropped his guard. "Okay, then. Sorry. I thought maybe *you* thought I'd led you on when you were vulnerable."

Scott grabbed his hand briefly before snatching it back. "No, never." He took a deep breath and let it out in a rush. "You're right about the nightmare. Something horrible happened and it's been messing with my head."

Scott's emotional pain was palpable. Seeing it, hearing it drip from every labored word, tugged at Kitt's heart. His childish beef with the man evaporated and his empathy took over. "I understand. A couple of your friends died." *Hassan with the missing beautiful face.* God, how petty of him to feel a spurt of jealousy over some poor dead guy.

Scott didn't respond immediately. He just kept staring at the ocean. "One friend, actually," he finally said. "J.J. We got through BUDs together, training buddies. There was something about him." He shook his head and flashed a grin. "We hit it off right away. He made me want to try harder, to succeed and not let him down. I'm not sure I would have made it all the way through without him."

"I bet you would have." It didn't seem possible that Scott needed anyone's help to be the tough, successful man that he was.

"Maybe," Scott allowed. "I just know that I felt extraordinarily lucky to have such a close friend to support and be supported by. Having him by my side gave me confidence. It was awesome when we ended up in the same team and could continue what I thought of as a strong partnership within the tight group of other guys. He always had my back, and I had his."

"You loved him." Kitt blurted out the observation before he could think better of it.

"Well, of course. I loved him like a brother."

No, not quite like that. It was an audacious thought, yet Kitt knew he was right. Everything about Scott—his expression, his tone of voice—confirmed it. "You trusted him," he said instead of anything more intimate, knowing that Scott wouldn't be open to facing, let alone admitting to, a closer bond.

"You have to trust everyone in the team. That's what makes us successful and helps keep us alive."

When Scott fell silent again, Kitt waged a war with himself before prompting for more. "You feel guilty because he died." It seemed obvious, so he made it more of a statement than a question.

To his surprise, Scott shook his head, then shifted to look at him. "No, not guilty, exactly. There was no way for me to have stopped what happened." He took a deep breath and let it out slowly. "We were having dinner in this little restaurant that we liked. It's never a good idea to develop habits when you're out there. It makes you vulnerable. But the area was as secure as anything can get in that part of the world, and we'd done a lot of work building up trust within the community.

"We never let our guard down completely but we were relaxed that night—laughing as we ordered because of something the waiter who always served us said."

"Hassan?" Kitt's stomach fluttered with anxiety. He knew he didn't really want to hear this story. Yet he also could appreciate that it was important to Scott to tell him. It was flattering that the man felt comfortable enough to do so when it was obviously a painfully raw effort.

A flash of emotion crossed Scott's eyes, a combination of anger and grief. "I spoke his name?"

"Yes." Kitt swallowed hard before forcing the next words out. "His face was disfigured."

The anger won out over the grief. Scott's eyes turned flinty, as if he were picturing what he wanted to do in retribution of the act of terrorism. "Yes," he ground out.

"*'His beautiful face,'*" Kitt dared to say in a hushed tone.

Scott shuddered before closing his eyes briefly and pressing his fingertips against them. "Yes." Dropping his hand, he stared straight at Kitt. "He was young, about your age. And his life had been so hard, most of it consumed by war—and still, he was hopeful." He grabbed a handful of wet sand and stared while it slipped through his fingers. "And he was gorgeous. You didn't have to be gay to appreciate that. He liked to flirt, too," he added with wistful smile.

"We went along with it because, why not? It's lonely in those long missions, especially when you get downtime. In those countries you're careful not to pay attention to any females. Forget politeness or respect… It's just too dangerous for them if their male relatives think they've been inviting scrutiny. We don't want to make their lives harder than they already are."

Scott's knuckles went white as he fisted the last grains of sand. "He should have been safe in his family's restaurant. He wasn't the target. We were, but because he was there with us and standing closest to J.J., he was killed, too. He would have left the table already if I hadn't kept chatting with him. Why didn't I just shut my fucking mouth and let him get on with his job?" Scott groaned, doubled over and pounded the sand between his legs. "That's what I feel guilty about."

There was too much agony in the man's words, and it pulsed out of him in waves that Kitt swore he could feel as much as the ocean breeze. He couldn't *not* offer comfort, and before he knew what he was doing, he lunged forward and grabbed Scott in a hug. He meant it purely as a gesture of friendship, and if he enjoyed the physical closeness more than he should, well he was going to have to forgive himself for it. So long as he didn't try to take things further, it was okay to be there for Scott.

It only took as long as necessary for Kitt to have that discussion inside his head until Scott responded by wrapping his arms around Kitt and hugged him back. From there it seemed almost natural for Kitt to end up sitting on Scott's lap. The heat of the man's body burned away the wetness from the sea, warming Kitt's ass and sending the wrong signals to his dick. Before he could consider how inappropriate that was, a hardness pressed against his hip. He wasn't the only one feeling the effects of their closeness. With his head nestled in the side of Scott's neck, he could swear he heard the pounding of the man's heart. His breathing was harsh as well, although whether that was from an effort to hold back tears or something else, Kitt didn't know. It was just so lovely being there with him, touching, drawing comfort from one another, and he didn't want to muddle the experience by trying to read into it more than what was in the offing.

A few seconds later, Scott broke the spell. Unlike the night before, he didn't toss Kitt away. Instead, he gently removed Kitt from his lap, rose to his feet and helped him do the same. Scott didn't try to hide his erection —

and neither did Kitt. They stood awkwardly for a moment, Scott staring once more out over the ocean and Kitt staring at him.

Finally, Scott returned his look. His expression was just short of grim before he mustered a smile. "Let's go back and make some pancakes. I'm starving from my run."

"Sure." Kitt turned toward the house without waiting for Scott to do so. He raised his chin to show he wasn't embarrassed by what had happened and how he'd reacted. He was tired of playing games.

Scott matched his stride. "How about I take you out to dinner? I know we've got a lot of food, but I am suddenly dying for lobster—and clams, corn on the cob, the whole nine yards. What do you say?"

Because the idea of going out with Scott, even for something as simple as a meal, made him happy, he didn't fight it or worry about the cost. "That sounds wonderful. Thank you."

"It's a date, then."

Scott seemingly didn't mean anything by those words. It was only an expression, yet Kitt couldn't help grinning. *Yes, it is.*

Chapter Seven

Scott didn't want to examine too closely his decision to take Kitt to the Crab Shack for dinner. Yes, Penny worked there, but it was also the best place for a shore dinner — and a person couldn't beat the prices. So, he hushed the voice inside his head telling him to leave and go somewhere else as he opened the door to usher Kitt inside the rambling building that had been a fixture in town since well before his own family had bought a house there. It was early, meaning that few people sat dotted around the main room.

They had decided on eating dinner around the time usually reserved for the elderly because, after returning from the beach, they'd enjoyed something of a brunch and had eaten nothing since. Scott had scarfed down pancakes, bacon and even strawberry shortcake with more gusto than he'd had recently for food. Something about his talk with Kitt concerning the horrors of his last deployment had lifted an invisible weight off him. He could almost breathe easier, and there was room in his stomach for more than the sourness of guilt.

Now he was just getting maudlin, perhaps. He wasn't into therapy and delving into his feelings. Yet, as he entered the cool, dark restaurant, he did feel lighter and happier than he had since he'd lost his best friend. A genuine smile broke out as he approached the hostess. He was determined that it would be a fun night. Kitt deserved it, not only because of the crap he'd been dealing with in his own life, but also because of the shit Scott had thrown at him in the last twelve-plus hours. Scott could only hope that this evening would be a sufficient way to say how sorry he was about the whipsaw events whereby he'd led the boy on, only to rebuff him strongly within seconds. He was lucky Kitt was such a forgiving kind of person.

By all rights, Kitt should be furious with him, yet out on the beach, he hadn't hesitated to offer comfort. It spoke volumes about the guy's magnanimous character. Scott's behavior, on the other hand, was nothing to be proud of. And it wasn't merely how he'd latched on to Kitt, literally, in the throes of a nightmare. Scott's head had been clear out on the beach, and still when Kitt had offered simple comfort, Scott had taken advantage of it. He could feel the light warmth of Kitt's ass on his lap, despite the hours that had elapsed. It had felt so right to put him there and hold him tight. So had the arousal that followed, and that was something Scott felt guilty about. He was giving Kitt mixed signals and that wasn't right. It was disturbing for him, at least— probably for Kitt, too.

And what did it say about him that he kept reacting this way to another man? Why had it felt like a lie when he'd said he loved J.J. as a brother? There was that shadowy thing in the corner of his mind that had lurked there for as long as he could remember.

Normally, he ignored it and it let him. But it had been kicking up a fuss these last few days, demanding to be heard. It scared him in some nameless way, making him think he was a coward. He knew he had to wrestle it under control, send it packing back to its rightful place while he picked up the pieces of his life and his career.

But he wasn't going to let his inner demon spoil the night—for Kitt's sake, if not his own. And so what if he put his hand on the small of his back while they walked toward the hostess' lectern? It was courtesy. He knew his way around this place and could detect a small tension in his guest, even without touching him. Being in public scared Kitt, if only a little. It was Scott's job to put him at ease. A second after his palm made contact with a spot just above Kitt's ass, the muscles there relaxed visibly, confirming that Scott had made the right call.

Before they reached the hostess, Penny swung around from the booth area to the left and strode over to them. Her face was lit with a welcoming smile that would make most men's pants feel like they'd shrunk. She was wearing the Crab Shack uniform of khaki shorts and a red polo shirt with the restaurant's logo on the breast. Penny's shorts barely met the definition of decent, being cut high and hugging her slender thighs like a second skin. Knowing the current owner of the place as he did, Scott understood that the waitstaff were given a lot of latitude in what they wore below the waist. Anything that brought in more business and higher tips was all to the good.

Scott made himself give those lovely legs a thorough look, because that was the whole point, yet frustratingly he was only mildly impressed. *Dude, what is your problem?* He rather worried that he had the answer to that question already.

Penny waved at the hostess. "I've got them, Jen. Please put them down for table five in my section." She refocused all her attention on Scott. "Hey there. I'm glad to see you took me up on my offer already." Her gaze flicked at Kitt. "Hi." Then she gazed at Scott's arm, the one connected to the hand touching Kitt's back.

Dropping his arm, Scott cleared his throat. "Hi, Penny. We decided a shore dinner was in order, and no one does it better than here."

Penny cocked a hip. "You've got that right. As early as it is, you've got no waiting and there's an ocean-view booth open. Come this way." She all but winked as she turned and sauntered farther into the restaurant. The way her luscious backside filled those shorts was a feast in and of itself.

But Scott barely took it in before he once more put his palm against Kitt's back to gently ease him to walk in front. Kitt's skinny jeans turned out to be far more provocative, easily winning the 'who wore it best' contest, one that had been created entirely by Scott's stupid brain. He forced himself to look across the room and out of the window facing the ocean. It was a fabulous night, and the sun hadn't quite started to set. Good as her word, Penny brought them to one of the best tables in the place. Scott waited until Kitt had slipped onto the bench seat on one side before taking the other.

Penny took out her ordering pad. "So, two shore dinners, right? I bet you want a double, huh, Scott?"

He nodded. "Yes, ma'am. How about you, Kitt?"

Kitt's gaze had been on the ocean. He shifted to look at first Penny, then Scott. "I don't know."

Scott mentally smacked himself. Of course he didn't. He'd bet Emilio, the fucker, had never treated Kitt to something like this, despite living in Boston. "A double comes with a quart of steamers, two one-and-a-quarter pound lobsters and two ears of corn, plus a mound of potato salad and cold slaw. The regular order is half of all of that," he added, somewhat lamely, as if that detail weren't hard-wired into the word 'double'. But he felt protective of Kitt, and somehow he couldn't quite stop treating him with kid gloves.

When I'm not teasing him with kisses and hard-ons before rejecting him. When did I become such an asshole?

Kitt grinned. "I definitely want the single portion version."

"Fair enough." Scott glanced at Penny to see that she was getting the order.

She treated him to a frank stare and a sexy smirk. "You want the usual Sam Adams, Scott?"

"That sounds great, thanks." An ice-cold beer would help take this ridiculous edge off.

Penny slowly changed her attention to Kitt. "If you want a beer, too, I'll have to card you. Restaurant policy, and no offense, but you don't look old enough to drink." There was a catty undertone that set Scott's teeth on edge.

If Kitt detected it, he didn't appear fazed. "I am, but I only want an unsweetened iced tea. Thanks."

"Sure. I'll put the orders in and be back in a second with those drinks." She brushed Scott's shoulder with her hand as she left. The touch did nothing for him, even though he really wanted it to.

He looked to see if Kitt had witnessed the brief interaction, but the boy practically had his nose pressed against the window. The Crab Shack was closer to the town center, so the marina was visible, as well as the ocean. For a few seconds, Scott simply sat and enjoyed watching Kitt admire the view. There was something so unabashedly open about his reactions. Kitt wore all his emotions on his sleeve, and despite what he'd been through, he had clearly not become jaded. No one would blame him if he had. Still, it was a hopeful sign for the rest of the species that someone could come through trauma and keep that wonder within them—to be able to see the good and beauty in the world.

Like Hassan.

That stray thought caused a stab of pain. He didn't think he reacted in any audible way, yet Kitt turned his face abruptly toward him.

"Are you okay?"

Scott forced a smile. "Sure."

Penny gave him time to pull himself together more by arriving with a tray of drinks. "Here you go, boys." She placed a glass of water in front of each of them before adding the beer and iced tea.

Scott grabbed his and chugged down half the glass. The cool liquid eased his tight throat, and the hit of liquor had an almost instant effect on his nerves. Or maybe he just wanted it to. "Thanks, Penny."

"I'll bring your chowder out in a sec." Again, she touched his shoulder as she left.

"Chowder? Did we order that?" Kitt asked with a frown.

"Oh, it comes with the meal, a cup for you and a bowl for me."

"Really? Wow, I'm not sure I'm going to manage even a single portion of the meal. Sounds like a lot of food."

"Nah, you'll be fine. It's been hours since we last ate."

Kitt rested his chin on his palm. "True. Good thing we ate dessert already. Plus," he added, casting his gaze downward, "the meal has to be expensive."

"Not really. This place has good prices. It's not going to break the bank, so don't worry about it," he added in a low, gentle tone. "And, there's always room for dessert. That's what my grandpa used to say. They have a great Indian pudding here."

"I've never had that."

"It's an old New England dessert made with cornmeal and molasses, served warm with vanilla ice cream on top."

Kitt grinned. "Ice cream, huh? I'll definitely have to try it."

"Good." They sat grinning at each other until Penny returned with the chowder.

She managed to lean way over as she placed his bowl in front of him. A whiff of her perfume caught his attention and there was a sparkle in her eyes. "Enjoy, boys." Scott made himself watch her walk away.

"She wants you." Kitt made the statement in a matter-of-fact voice while he dumped his packet of oyster crackers into his chowder then stared at it as he pressed them down with his spoon to absorb some of the liquid.

Scott suppressed a sigh and did the same with his food. "Yeah, she's not subtle. Never has been, come to think of it. I had to be careful when I was around her years ago. Classic case of a little girl's crush on a teenage boy."

Kitt swallowed a spoonful of chowder. "I can relate. As a middle school kid, I used to watch the high school boys practice out on the fields. It didn't matter which sport. There was always something to admire, even though I knew they were out of my league *and* playing for the wrong team." He shrugged. "Most of them were, I assume. There was no way to tell. Where I come from, other than a few girls who were openly lesbian—and who got a lot of harassment—being out and proud wasn't a thing."

"Yeah, I bet it is extra hard for gay kids," Scott allowed. The nostalgia took over. "It's the same for everyone to some degree, though, isn't it? For me it was Tracy Katz." He took a big spoonful of chowder and chased it down with more beer. The combination was as close to heaven as he could imagine. "I was in eighth grade, and she was in tenth. Only two years' difference, but at that age, it may as well have been decades. She was an unattainable older woman, and I was undoubtedly just some pimply little kid to her."

"I bet she wouldn't think that now," Kitt said over the rim of his glass.

Scott shrugged. "True, my face has cleared up considerably."

Kitt giggled, making Scott grin in return. They didn't speak for a while as they quickly finished up the chowder. When he was scraping the bottom of his cup, Kitt said, "Anyway, Penny's all grown up and she's sending some pretty strong signals." He glanced at Scott, "I can Lyft back to the cottage once we've finished eating."

"Thanks, but I'm sure Penny is working until closing time."

"They have a bar. You could wait for her."

The obvious answer, the correct one based on Scott's experience, was "Thanks, bro." He only shook his head. "No, it's fine. Maybe I'll ask her out later."

"How are you doing here?" Penny arrived laden with a tray full of their dinner. Her obvious strength in carrying the heavy burden was admirable, as was the efficient way she laid it all out. "Another round of drinks?" When he and Kitt nodded, she scooped up the empty glasses along with the dirty dishes and sashayed away.

Scott's attention was back on Kitt before she'd disappeared from sight. "Need any help?" Even as he asked the question, he saw that Kitt didn't. The boy was already stripping the first clam of its skin, then its stomach.

"You only eat the necks?" Scott wasn't surprised. The world was divided into two types of people, those who ate clam stomachs along with the clam necks and those who didn't, although there was rumored to be a mysterious third group that ate only the stomachs.

Kitt dipped the clam into the hot water. "I can eat them when they're fried, but not steamed." He made a face. "Too mealy." He plopped the clam into the butter before picking up another one.

"Ah, you're a hoarder who eats a bunch at a time." This was another marker that separated humanity — those who ate clams one at a time versus those who piled them up in the butter first.

Scott dug into his bucket. "Well, I'm a whole clam man myself and like to savor each one individually." So saying, he quickly cleaned his clam, soaked it in butter and plopped it into his mouth. "Hmm." *Simple and yet amazingly good.*

"One more reason why it would never work between us," Kitt observed. "I mean, in addition to that gay versus straight problem." He froze for a second, as if realizing what he'd said, then his cheeks bloomed pink.

Scott moved quickly to ease his embarrassment. "Um, I don't know. The divide between the proper way to eat steamers is a wide one to bridge. I think sexuality is more fluid." He winked and felt foolish, except Kitt visibly relaxed and kept cleaning his clams.

Their conversation trailed off while they ate. It was companionable silence, not awkward at all. They steadily worked their way through the clams, then the corn. Melted butter slid down Kitt's chin, making him snort. He swiped at it with the back of his hand in order to keep munching through the ear of corn, making an even bigger mess. Scott couldn't help chuckling. The whole thing reminded him of how often the same thing had happened to him when he'd been a child. Even though Kitt was an adult, there was a lot of the kid left in him, the joyful part that found pleasure in simple things. Scott marveled again at how resilient the guy was. Watching him eat was the best part of the meal.

He felt a little disappointed when Kitt didn't need his help eating the lobster. Karen had been the first person to introduce him to it, according to Kitt, and had given him a crash course in breaking open the shell and digging out the meat. Ridiculous, really, but Scott wished he'd had the pleasure. He settled, instead, on taking in the show, although he tried not to be too obvious about the attention he was paying. The only interruption to their quiet dinner was Penny popping over with irritating regularity to see if they wanted another round of drinks or anything else. Normally, he would have appreciated the attentive service. This night, he just wanted to be left alone — alone with Kitt, that was. He knew his focus on the boy was rude and kind of creepy, yet he couldn't help doing it. His own meal didn't suffer, in any event. He was on autopilot and had plowed through his food before he knew it.

Kitt sat back, sucking on a lobster leg. "I'm stuffed," he said, pulling the chewed stick of shell out of his mouth. "Sorry... I don't think I can manage another bite. I'll have to try Indian pudding another time."

Scott drained his third glass of beer before answering with a pat on his stomach. "I'm full, too. We'll come back another time and start with dessert. How does that sound?"

"Yum, although we have so much food left at home. The cottage, I mean. I'm not sure it will make sense to eat out again in the few days we're going to be together." Kitt's gaze skittered toward the window. "I really need to start thinking of going."

Alarm shot through Scott, making his heart race and his full stomach tighten as if he were in the middle of a firefight. "No!" He winced with the force of his response. When Kitt turned a startled expression on him, he softened his tone. "I mean, you don't have to worry about that yet. I have more than a week's worth of leave left, but you know I don't mind sharing the cottage with you."

Kitt gave him a shy smile. "I know."

The look and the sweet timbre of his voice was like a punch to the gut...and lower. Even though he should have been used to it at that point, the reaction still caught him by surprise. Everything increased — his heartbeat, his breathing, the cramping in his stomach. This was crazy. He was not gay or bi or anything other than strictly straight. That issue had been resolved with extreme prejudice years ago. *The. End.* He did not want Kitt. *No way.* This was some kind of hyped-up older brother nonsense messing with his head. He wanted to help Kitt, not fuck him. He needed to get his shit together, because it wasn't only himself that he was hurting with this seesaw of emotion and desire. The mixed signals he was throwing Kitt's way were just another version of abuse. He wasn't going to be one more guy taking out his anger and insecurities on the poor kid.

"Wow, you guys destroyed your dinners." A super-cheery Penny popped up seemingly out of nowhere.

It was the perfect timing. Seeing someone he should be focusing his attention on, Scott grabbed the opportunity, almost with desperation. He turned on the charm. "Yeah, we did. It was amazing, as usual."

Penny flashed a dimpled smile. "Thanks, I'll let the chef know. Room for dessert?"

Scott rolled his eyes. "No, ma'am." He patted his stomach, liking how Penny's gaze tracked the movement. Despite the huge meal, his six-pack was in its usual impressive condition. "No more room. I'll take the check, though."

"Sure thing." She grabbed a few dishes from the table before leaving.

This time, Scott kept his gaze fixed on her until she'd left his line of sight before he returned his focus to Kitt. The guy had a knowing look on his face, and there was a hint of something in his eyes that Scott chose to ignore because it had a sadness to it. For one mad second, Scott wanted to jettison his burgeoning plan for the night and simply take Kitt home for a quiet evening in front of the TV.

Man, are you fucked up. You know what you need to do. Stop being an idiot.

He cleared his throat briefly before saying, "Look... I'm going to take you back, then return here to wait for Penny to get off work, the way you suggested," he added, because he was that much of a jerk, apparently. "That's assuming she wants me to."

For a brief, heartbreaking moment, it seemed as if tears pooled in Kitt's eyes before he blinked them away. "Of course she does." He *tsked*. "Seriously, you're not worried about me, are you? I'll be fine on my own."

Scott nodded. "Yeah, sure you will." It felt as if he should say more, but before he could think of what, Kitt slid out of his seat.

"I'll head out to the car so I don't cramp your style."

Relief coursed through him at how easy Kitt was making things for him, then guilt chased after it. He ignored that and got to his feet. "Okay. No, wait. Wait by the hostess' station. Please." He was being overly cautious, but he didn't want Kitt outside at night alone.

Kitt didn't kick up a fuss. "Sure."

Scott made himself not watch the guy walk away. Instead, he hunted for Penny and found her creating a bill at the computer toward the back.

"Oh, hi, Scotty. I was coming to you."

He forced a smile, kicking himself to get his head in the game. "I wanted to save you the trouble." Holding out his credit card, he added, "And I was hoping you're free after your shift ends tonight?"

Penny's movements didn't falter as she flashed him a megawatt smile. "I thought you'd never ask. Frankly, you know, I was beginning to think you were on a date or something."

Scott felt his face warm and forced is body to relax. "Huh! No. Kitt's a friend of Karen's. We happen to be sharing the cottage at the moment. I'm just being a good host."

Penny handed him the slip to sign. "You were always a good guy, Scott. Not too good, I hope," she added with a sultry look.

Scott added in a generous tip before signing it. "We'll have to see, won't we?" He stared straight into her pretty eyes that seemed for a second to be the wrong color for him. "What time should I be back?"

"Whenever you want. The restaurant closes an hour before the bar. I'll meet you there, so long as you promise not to drink too much. I'm counting on you functioning at full SEAL strength."

He chuckled with less enthusiasm than he wanted. This was the kind of hot, if silly, banter that was a prelude to a fantastic time. "No worries. I'll stick to soda for the rest of the night. I know how to prepare for a mission."

"I bet you do." Blowing an air kiss at him, Penny sauntered back to work.

Telling himself that he was a lucky man, Scott headed for the front door. A spurt of relief coupled with warmth knocked the cockiness out of him when he saw that Kitt was waiting right where he'd asked him to. He clenched his fingers for a few seconds before deliberately relaxing them. He was being ridiculous. His evening was shaping up just fine. It had been months since he'd been laid and there was no reason for him to feel so conflicted.

"Let's go," he said as he reached Kitt.

"Are you sure you don't want me to get a Lyft back instead?"

Scott shook his head. "Nah. It's early still. Penny won't be free for a few hours. Plus, I want to, um, clean up a bit."

"Oh, right." Kitt turned toward the door.

Scott reached out to put his hand on him as he had before and had to snatch it back. Kitt wasn't his date. He was a grown man who could walk to the car without aid or guidance. Scott's time would be better spent planning out how he was going to handle his date with Penny. As strong as her signals were, he wasn't going to act like this was all about dipping his dick as quickly as possible. Penny deserved better than that, even though they were both only looking for a hook-up.

The ride back to the cottage was quiet. Scott couldn't think of anything to say and Kitt didn't seem inclined to chat, either. Once inside, Scott went to take a quick shower and change his clothes. He didn't have many choices with him, but at least he could change into a polo shirt and khakis. Thanks to Kitt's amazing shave, it didn't take much to smooth his cheeks again. As he stood looking at himself in the bathroom mirror, he suffered a weird moment where his face didn't look familiar to him. For a few seconds, it was as if his entire existence were surreal, a fiction of his own making.

"Jesus, you're losing your shit, Carpenter." He could almost hear J.J.'s voice instead of his own. His friend had always been great at calling Scott's bullshit and putting him back on the right track. "Stop overthinking this."

He ran his fingers through his hair, then returned to his room to grab some condoms. There weren't any in his bag. No surprise. He'd packed quickly on his way back home and having sex hadn't been on his mind at all. No matter. There was a gas station on the way that he could stop at, and it would kill some time. It was still pretty early, and he didn't relish the idea of spending too long sitting at the bar, nursing a soda. He trotted downstairs and found Kitt on the couch, watching television. For one mad second, he wanted to go join him.

He curled his toes and planted himself at the bottom of the stairs. "Hey. I'm heading out."

Kitt glanced over his shoulder. "Okay. Have fun." The boy's voice sounded strained.

Scott hesitated before reaching for his keys on the counter. He jingled them a few times. "I, um, might not be home again tonight. Are you okay with that?"

Kitt didn't bother looking at him as he responded. "Sure. I figured as much." Then he did twist his head to stare over his shoulder. "I'll be fine, Scott. Really. Go have fun. You…you need this."

Scott dropped his gaze, unable to look at Kitt's earnest face. "Yeah, I guess I do." He looked over at him again. "But you call me if anything happens that worries you. Anything at all. Understand?"

Kitt smiled briefly. "Aye, aye, sir."

Scott nodded. "Good." Then he strode out of the house before he could talk himself out of it.

* * * *

"Another Coke?"

Scott turned his attention from the television above the bar to the bartender. "No, thanks. I'm swimming in the stuff." His time waiting for Penny had been longer and more boring than he'd expected. The game playing wasn't interesting enough to keep his attention.

Instead, he kept imagining what Kitt was watching. Tension mounted in him with each passing minute, as well. He'd already been walking into the restaurant before he remembered that he and Kitt hadn't exchanged mobile numbers. The landline at the cottage was long gone. So, the first thing he'd done was text Karen to have her give his number to Kitt. He wasn't exactly sure where his sister had found the emoji that she'd sent back, but it made her displeasure abundantly and profanely clear. It had flayed his already-sensitive nerves. And with three beers already under his belt from dinner, he didn't dare drink any more alcohol to take the edge off.

Penny sauntered up. She'd taken time to swing by his way every so often, despite the busy night the restaurant was having. "Almost done." Her eyes flashed as she left.

"You're a lucky bastard," the bartender observed. "Many have tried, and all have failed. Penny is picky."

Scott grinned, or maybe he grimaced. "I have no doubt. She and I go way back."

"Uh-huh. Somehow, I don't think nostalgia is the deciding factor here." The man gave Scott a blatant once-over before going to help another customer.

Scott didn't need the reminder from anyone about how the physique necessary for a special operator in the military gave him a certain attraction. Despite their history, he wouldn't have been surprised if Penny had given him a polite brush-off if he'd ended up an overweight engineer or something. Her childhood crush was undoubtedly fueled by the common fascination with the danger he represented, too. That was fine. This evening was all about physical pleasure, a relief valve from the pressure he was under. He truly believed it was the same for her. She was bored with her life, dissatisfied with her job and still curious about what it would be like to have him. Neither of them was looking for more. If he thought for a moment that she was, he would put the brakes on right then and there.

"Okay, I'm free." Penny caught him by surprise, her bag slung over one shoulder, more heat in her eyes.

Scott stood. "That was fast."

She trailed a finger down his arm. "I had good incentive."

Because he felt a sudden urge to move away from the touch, he leaned into it instead. "Would you like to go somewhere else for a drink?"

She gave a little laugh. "You know the sidewalks around here have already started to roll up. How about you follow me back to my place? I have wine and beer. And you can drink, too," she added in a lower voice, "given that you don't have to drive again until morning."

The almost purring timber of her tone made his cock stir, which gave him a sense of relief. Leaning in closer, he said, "Sounds like a plan."

"Great. Let's go."

He followed her out of the restaurant and made sure she was safely in her car before heading to his rental. She was right about the town closing early. There was little traffic as they drove to her place, a small townhouse-style apartment complex, a few miles away. He parked in a spot marked 'visitor' near where she pulled in. It was farther away from the door than he would have liked. As he went first to her, then to her place, he scanned the area, looking for trouble.

"Can't turn it off, huh?" He glanced at her with a frown. "You're acting like we're in a war zone."

"Oh, yeah." He chuckled. "You're right. It's second nature." His estimation of the woman rose in that moment. She was smart and sensitive, and the reminder gave him pause and doubt about his assumptions.

As she reached into her purse for her keys, he stayed her hand. "Look. I, um, want to make sure we're on the same page."

She quirked her lips. "Come on, Scott. This isn't an *Officer and a Gentleman* kind of thing. I want to fulfill a fantasy, and the fact that you don't live around here makes it an easy decision. I'm still trying to figure out my life, but it doesn't hinge on marrying Mr. Right. Frankly, I'm not sure he even exists. What I am sure about is that I want to get you in my bed for the night. And you don't have to stay over if you don't want to. In fact, it will save me the trouble of washing my face and brushing my teeth before you wake."

Her directness surprised him. "You don't have to pretend with me, Penny."

"Right back at you, Scotty."

Surprised again, he responded, "I'm not and I won't."

Penny raised her eyebrows and stared at him for a few seconds before closing the gap and kissing him. It was everything he expected — soft and inviting, with a passion that built slowly as she slid one arm around his waist and pressed against his body. He did the same, hugging her close, taking the lead. He slid his tongue between her pliant lips and tasted the sweet warmth of her mouth. His dick hardened, as it should, as he'd wanted it to. The feeling of it constrained within his pants made him bolder. He sucked on her tongue, practically inhaling her. Penny moaned in response.

And that was when the spell broke, just as it had back in the cottage. This time his movements were more controlled. He gently broke the kiss and slowly held her at a distance, his hands on her arms, rubbing them with his thumbs as if to soothe the hurt he was about to cause. She kept her eyes closed for a few seconds, long enough for his mind to play tricks on him. Her hair was in a messy ponytail, but it was the wrong color. Her beautiful, delicate face kept changing shape in his mind's eye to conform to the one he wanted to see. Her arms were actually too muscular and at the same time, she had too many curves.

Her eyes fluttered open and she gazed at him with a knowing look. "I'm not who you want to be with, am I?"

Scott swallowed hard. "I…"

"It's okay." She moved away, causing his arms to drop, before opening her door. "I saw how you looked at him over dinner. I'm not naïve, Scott, just hopeful."

He couldn't bring himself to deny it. "I'm sorry." It was lame, yet all he had.

"Me, too. It's okay, though. Really. I have enough self-respect to want to be the center of attention when I'm in bed with a man. Go home and don't worry about me. I'm fine."

"Thank you," he managed, although his words were so inadequate. He felt like a heel and a coward.

"Don't worry," she said as she stepped into her apartment. "I'm not going to blab about this to anyone. It's no one else's business."

He opened his mouth to thank her again, but the door was already shutting in his face with a soft, dismissive click. He wasted only a few seconds more before sprinting to his SUV. Resolve was building within him. It was long past time to do what he clearly wanted, a side of himself he needed to explore, even if it was hard for him to accept.

The trade-off of being a SEAL over having a private life had always been enough, but damn, he was tired of fighting what came naturally. And nothing to date had felt more natural, more fulfilling, than being with Kitt. Refusing to accept this innate part of who he was, suppressing it and denying it even to himself, had been more than expedient. It had been cowardly. What did he care what others thought of him personally, so long as he remained the excellent operator that he'd become? His time in the field with the Teams was going to come to an end...and soon. He'd willingly given almost all his aging body could handle. Didn't he deserve to retire into a life he wanted when the time came? With whom he wanted? And he'd wanted Kitt from the first moment he'd seen him. Denying that had been like trying to swim against the tide. There were times when doing that was necessary and right. This wasn't one of them.

The only question was whether it was too late to give in to what he so desperately wanted.

Chapter Eight

Kitt didn't even try to go to sleep. He lay in his bed, listening to the sound of the waves crashing against the shore. Even with the air conditioner on, nature easily made enough noise to work its way inside the house and give him an almost musical backdrop to his misery. He was being utterly foolish, but no amount of rational discussion with himself was making a difference. He was lonely and jealous and missed Scott's presence in the house, even though he knew the man wasn't ever going to end up in this part of it…with him. In his bed. Making love to him the way he was doing with Penny Perfect right at the moment. Or maybe they were in pre-game mode, drinking on her couch, or maybe in his SUV. No, no way Scott would resort to a quick car-fuck instead of taking her home. He was nicer than that. A good man.

Unlike Kitt, who lay on top of his covers, staring at the ceiling and wishing for something he couldn't have. Instead of being grateful that Scott had taken the time and spent the money treating Kitt to a marvelous dinner, he was working up resentment with the kind of 'green-eyed monster' mindset that Emilio had always used as an excuse for his behavior. Thank God there was no one to witness it and he had all night to get his shit under control. Scott didn't deserve to return home to the hot mess Kitt had turned into. And staying awake had the bonus of easing his fears. After spending a few nights in the cottage alone, he'd thought he'd gotten past them. Having Scott sleeping down the hall had allowed him to truly relax. With him gone, every creak and groan of the old house caused his heartbeat to skip and his stomach to clench. He had to work to remind himself that Emilio had no idea where he was. He was safe, if more unhappy than he had been since arriving.

The sound of an engine outside mocked his reassurance a second later. He sat bolt upright and strained to hear more. Maybe it had been his imagination, but no. Those were definitely footsteps he'd heard on the stairs. Panic mounting within him, he slid off the bed as far from the door as he could get and looked around for anything he could use as a weapon. He'd kept a broom under the bed as the only thing he thought would help him if worst came to worst, but with Scott's arrival, he'd put it back in the kitchen closet. Now, he had nothing.

"Kitt, it's just me. Scott."

Those words sent him slumping against the bed, relief coursing through him, leaving him almost shaking. *What the fuck? Scott should be in Penny's...arms, not here.*

"Sorry... I would have called before returning, but when I asked Karen to text you my number, I forgot to ask her for yours." Scott was speaking right outside the bedroom door now. "May I come in?"

Kitt hesitated only a second before nodding, then realized Scott couldn't see. "Y-yes."

The hinges creaked as they opened, a kind of natural warning system that Kitt hadn't tried to fix when he'd arrived. Scott stood inside the frame, almost indistinct from the shadows. The sight of him still made Kitt's heart jump, though not from fear this time.

"Why did you come back?" he couldn't help asking before Scott said another word.

The man stepped closer, his face clearer now. He didn't look happy. "I, ah, realized I didn't want to be with Penny. She did too, actually, and was amazingly gracious about it."

Kitt got fully back on the bed and drew up his knees, conscious of how he was wearing only his underwear. "Why not? She's really pretty and sexy."

Scott came up to the other side of the bed and nodded. "Yes, she is. And she also deserves someone in her bed who is thinking only of her and how lucky he is that she's let him in."

"And that wasn't you?"

Scott shook his head again, slowly, his gaze boring a hole in Kitt. Then he held out his hand and said, "She's not the one I wanted to be with."

Kitt wasn't certain what Scott was saying or what he was offering. Obviously, it was hard for the man to say the words out loud. And what would those words be, exactly? *I'm closeted or I'm bi for the right guy?* Whatever it was, clearly the man had decided to push aside his 'I'm strictly straight' line, at least for this night. His gesture as well as the heated look in his eyes, however, were clear enough. He wanted Kitt to take that hand, probably to lead him to the bigger bed Scott had been sleeping in. There was no way the two of them could share the narrow single one Kitt currently sat on. The invitation for sex sure as hell made more sense than thinking Scott wanted him to come watch TV.

Kitt had a choice to make. Either he could allow Scott to take him to bed with the clear expectation that the man might never be able to own up to his sexuality, whatever it was, or he could pass. Something had led to this unexpected turn of events. It wasn't drunkenness, of that Kitt was sure. But whatever it was, would it last beyond this one night? Come morning, could Scott face and accept what had happened? If he dismissed it as some aberration, he would hurt Kitt more than any man ever had. The only way to prevent that was to order Scott to leave and let the opportunity die on the vine.

It was a hard decision to make, and yet at the same time, incredibly easy. A short period of misery was better than a lifetime of regret if he didn't take the chance. Placing his hand in Scott's, he let him tug him off the bed and lead him down the hall. Inside the master bedroom, Scott kissed him by the door. It was almost sweet, the passion boiling under the surface. And it held greater power because, unlike previous times, Scott had done it while sober, with no fugue state to blame it on. The slight contact made Kitt feel both welcome and safe, while hinting at what was to come. He got hard in an instant, and when Scott drew him in against his body, he felt the man's matching erection. A frisson of anticipation shot up his spine.

He let Scott set the pace, liking it when a man took charge of him, but also understanding that this was difficult for Scott. Kitt was certain that he'd never made love with another man before. There was undoubtedly some part of Scott that was freaking out, trying to put on the brakes. Kitt didn't want to contribute any power to that demon and call a stop to this wonderful time before it barely got started. And it might still end as the other times had, with Scott pushing him aside and aborting the entire thing. If that did happen again, it would gut Kitt, but he'd known that two minutes ago when he'd taken Scott's hand.

Fortunately, Scott was a masterful kisser. His efforts did a great job of making Kitt's brain fuzzy and killing his thoughts. As the kiss progressed to full mouth penetration, Scott started to disrobe without breaking the connection except for the second needed to get the shirt over his head. He also somehow managed to herd Kitt closer to the bed. With mounting anticipation, Kitt kicked himself into gear, helping Scott by unbuttoning the man's pants and slipping them past his hips. Then there was nothing between his hands and Scott's muscular ass. He cupped and squeezed, making him groan.

That made Kitt smile. He liked having that effect on Scott…on any man. He knew, as well, that there was a tantalizing hard dick inches away. But he didn't dare make a grab for it, fearing the move might be too much, too soon, for a newly awakened desire for another man. Sad as it was, he suspected Scott needed to keep some illusion that he was making love with a woman. The proof was in the way Scott managed to keep their groins from pressing against each other. For this first time, Kitt could live with that restriction. He didn't want to push Scott harder than he was ready to take things, so that meant keeping himself in check and continuing to let Scott lead them to the next step.

His legs hit the side of the bed, and Scott gently tumbled them onto it. At the same time, he pulled Kitt's underwear down and off with a brisk movement. Kitt immediately broke the kiss to turn onto his stomach in an effort to help Scott with whatever fantasy he was spinning in his head. Nothing screamed louder that he was fucking another man than seeing an erection.

"No," Scott murmured as he rolled Kitt onto his back. Kitt opened his eyes and in the gloom, he saw Scott staring at him. "You don't have to hide yourself. I see you, Kitt. I see *you*. There's no image of a woman floating in my head. I know I'm in bed with a man and I don't need to pretend otherwise. I want to make love to you face-to-face…if that's a thing, I mean."

Kitt could hear the insecurity in Scott's tone and understood that in some ways, Kitt was going to have to be the one in charge this night. He cupped Scott's cheek and stroked it with his thumb. "Yes, it's a thing — one that I love, actually."

"Good to know." Scott kissed him again, gliding his lips over Kitt's with a slow sweep before begging entrance with his tongue once more. At the same time, he placed his hand over Kitt's cock and clasped it, tentatively as first, then with greater pressure. "Just so we're clear, I'm new to this. I'm counting on your telling me when I'm getting it right or wrong. Be honest with me, *please*."

Kitt's breath hitched from the touch and he bucked into the hold. "Always," he managed to cough out before moaning.

Scott's teeth flashed in the gloom. "I want to be inside you, if that's okay." Kitt could only reply with a nod and another moan. "Don't come too soon, though. Let's make this last as long as we can." Scott's words were emphasized by him working his fingers along Kitt's shaft, tugging and massaging.

Kitt nodded again before frantically trying to stave off his orgasm. It had been a while since he'd enjoyed sex and hadn't had much control over his body even before. His balls were already tightening, and he feared he was going to disappoint his newfound lover by spoiling the fantasy of prolonged lovemaking. Not that he couldn't come again, of course, but it seemed important that he hold off until Scott was embedded within him before giving in to the need to come. He shuddered and arched his back, then felt the orgasm stopped in its tracks by a hard squeeze at the base of his dick.

Scott chuckled. "Not yet, sweetheart." He kissed Kitt once more, slowly tracing his lips before plunging his tongue into Kitt's willing mouth.

Kitt reached up to cling to the man's shoulders and pull him closer. Scott's hard cock slid against Kitt's hip, hot and solid, testament to how much Scott wanted him. It was thick and long and Kitt's hole clenched at the thought of being filled by it. Hooking one leg over Scott's, he tried to close the small gap between their bodies. Scott groaned down his throat, the vibration shooting straight to Kitt's trapped dick. He tried to maneuver himself to lift his ass in invitation, but Scott was too big and heavy for him to gain any measure of control.

Scott broke the kiss and peppered Kitt's face with short pecks before saying, "Easy, baby. I want to make sure I do this right, and as much as I want to slide inside you, I don't want it to hurt."

Kitt both appreciated the concern and felt frustrated by the delay. "It's okay. I'm ready for you." Whatever bite of pain that might come from an abrupt entry was worth it to him. His need for Scott had become too great for him to wait any longer.

With another quick kiss, Scott let go and rolled off the bed. Kitt couldn't keep the cry of dismay from bursting out. "It's okay. I'll just be a moment." Kitt fisted the sheets as he watched Scott rummage through his pants' pocket. He held a packet of condoms and a tiny bottle of lube as he returned. "I think part of me always knew where I'd end up this evening," he said, showing the lube to Kitt.

He knelt at Kitt's side while he sheathed his cock, then covered it all with slick. He moved closer and placed a hand on Kitt's thigh. "Tell me what to do."

Kitt smiled and kept his gaze on Scott as he raised his legs and held on to his knees. "Come between them and use a couple of fingers to coat me inside."

Scott wordlessly did as Kitt had instructed. He didn't hesitate, but there was something in his demeanor that telegraphed his lack of confidence. Emotion welled up in Kitt, a strong desire to make this night something special for Scott, a sense of caretaking and more… It frightened him to explore it too closely. So, putting it aside, he focused on the practical, knowing that what he did for Scott in this first exploration of his sexuality would impact the guy for the rest of his life—and maybe with future male lovers, although the thought of Scott with another man hurt. He shoved that away, as well.

When Scott had settled between Kitt's splayed legs, Kitt raised his hips more to give him easy access to his hole. "Squeeze some lube on two fingers and press them inside." It could have been a classroom tutorial on YouTube, except for the breathless quality of his voice.

Good military man that he was, Scott complied with the orders, squeezing a large amount of lube onto his fingers before tossing the tube aside. Then, with only a slight hesitation, he pressed the tips against Kitt's hole, teasing the flesh there with slow circles before slipping them inside. Kitt tensed for only a second before relaxing and welcoming the invasion. It helped to keep his eyes open, so that he could be constantly reminded of whom he was with. This was Scott, a wonderful man who cared about his wellbeing. If he told him to stop, he had no doubt that Scott would immediately. If he told him to pull out and leave him alone entirely, he knew that Scott wouldn't hesitate to do so. He wouldn't accuse Kitt of being a tease or a slut. Scott was an honorable man.

How could he not trust him? How could he not love him?

No, wait. Don't go there! Don't be greedy. One night. That's all you can count on.

His self-admonishment ended abruptly as his brain short-circuited because Scott had eased his fingers fully inside Kitt's ass, brushing his prostate. "Shit!" He closed his eyes and fisted the sheets with all his strength in an effort to hold back an orgasm.

"Like that, do you?" Scott's tone held both amusement and pride. A second later, he gripped the base of Kitt's cock, strangling the orgasm.

Kitt pounded the bed in frustration, those fingers inside him driving him crazy, while the ones around his dick did as well in an entirely different way. Scott only chuckled and kept stroking him slowly. With each swipe of his prostate, Kitt's pleasure sparked, his hole clenching then relaxing. Soon, he felt as if he couldn't stand the delay another moment.

"Please, Scott, fuck me. Come on. I'm ready."

Scott plunged his fingers deep inside Kitt's ass one more time, scissoring them in a move right out of *Anal Sex 101*. Kitt didn't need this much prep, but it was more about Scott at the moment. The man wouldn't enjoy his experience if he thought he was hurting Kitt. It was important to not push him further than he was ready for. Finally, he pulled his fingers out with one last, long, slow drag. Kitt moaned in appreciation and opened his eyes the moment he felt what had to be the head of Scott's cock preparing to enter him. He wanted to see the expression on his lover's face when he breached another man for the first time.

Scott didn't disappoint. His gaze fixed on Kitt's, Scott leaned forward. His broad shaft stretched Kitt wide enough to make him wince. Scott stopped immediately. "Am I hurting you?"

How to explain this? "Yes," Kitt bit out, "in a good way. Please don't stop."

Scott only hesitated for a moment before surging forward to seat himself balls deep. His eyes slammed shut. "Jesus, you're so tight."

Kitt giggled before closing his own eyes and relaxing into the bed. "My superpower. Now, fuck me, hard, fast."

Scott's breath tickled his ear. "Is that what you really want?"

By way of an answer, Kitt squeezed his hole as tight as he could and wrapped his legs around Scott's, his heel against the man's muscular ass. That was all the encouragement Scott needed. He pulled his cock almost completely out before thrusting it back in again. Then he set a pace that sent sparks flying to Kitt's dick, and at the same time, Scott released his death grip around the shaft to stroke instead. The orgasm hit Kitt with a ferocity that had him throwing back his head and howling. He let go of the sheets to dig his nails into Scott's shoulders. He wanted to keep as many connections to the man as he could. Cum splashed on his stomach, and at the same time, Scott's dick swelled and pulsed inside him. A roar drowned out Kitt's own dying mewling. Then a heavy weight came down onto him and hot breath panted into his hair. Kitt held on to Scott's sweaty body, never wanting to let him go.

* * * *

The sex had been off the charts, but the amazing part of the night was that Scott held him in his arms as they lay in bed. Once the high of coming had dissipated, Kitt had braced himself for Scott's regret. He hadn't expected the man to do anything as hurtful as to throw him out of bed, but he had assumed Scott would put distance between them as he came to grips with what he'd done. That concern had appeared to manifest when Scott had disengaged their bodies and left the bedroom entirely. But he'd been back quickly, a warm washcloth in his hand that he'd used to clean Kitt with a gentle care that nearly made Kitt cry. Then he'd been back in bed, covering them both with a sheet and pulling Kitt into the safety of his arms.

Neither of them had slept yet. At least Kitt hadn't, and although Scott was still and quiet, there was none of the heavy breathing associated with sleep. And Scott's fingers occasionally skittered along Kitt's arm, a slight yet deliberate touch. Kitt had to bite his tongue to keep from asking questions. He wanted to make sure Scott was okay, that he had no regrets. But the idea of speaking raised the fear of breaking the spell that they seemed to have woven together. He'd take lying silently against Scott's chest, hearing his heartbeat, feeling the rise and fall of his chest for the rest of the night, rather than risking its loss by demanding too much. In the end, Scott proved to be both smart and the braver man.

"I'm not freaked out, you know."

Kitt smiled against his chest. "I'm glad to hear that."

"I just wanted to make sure you know." He shifted slightly so that they almost faced each other. A hardness bumped against Kitt's hip. "I think I'm going to want to do it again in the next little while if that's okay with you, if you're not sore or anything."

Kitt pressed a kiss to the man's pec. "No, I'm not."

That wasn't strictly true. His hole throbbed from its recent invasion, but his dick also pulsed at the idea of being fucked again. It was like the early days of his new adult life as a gay man, when his libido had gotten the better of him. It didn't matter. In some ways he felt as if this was a new beginning for him. And he also knew that if he needed to switch gears to oral or manual sex, Scott wouldn't demand more. It was simply wonderful that Scott was thinking of 'again' instead of running screaming from him.

Scott kissed him on the top of his head, the casual affection saying more than the request to fuck another time. "Don't say or do anything just because you think I want it. It's critical to me that we're honest with each other. Okay?"

"Of course." Kitt lifted his head and, using Scott's chest for leverage, looked at him. Scott's gaze met his. "And that also means that if you want tonight to be a one-off thing, that's fine." He looked away. "Disappointing, but I won't make a fuss. I know this must be hard for you."

Scott cupped the side of Kitt's face, forcing him to look him in the eye once more. "It's not, actually. Being here with you, making love, is one of the easiest, most natural things I've ever done. I'd never had sex with a man before, but that doesn't mean I hadn't thought about it. Once I accepted my attraction to you, the doubt and confusion fell away." He slid his thumb across Kitt's lips. "I'm bisexual, and finally acknowledging that is freeing, not scary."

Kitt stretched forward to kiss him. He meant for it to be comforting…or even playful. Scott turned it smoldering, and before Kitt knew it, he was on his back with Scott ravaging his mouth. Their equally hard cocks brushed against each other with a maddeningly slow friction. With a whimper, he tried to roll Scott on top of him, almost desperate to have him inside his ass once more. Scott resisted, and instead clasped both dicks in his large hand and jerked them in unison. Kitt got with the program quickly, intent on coming no matter how it happened. The feel of the hot shaft against his, the pulsing of it as Scott came, sent him over the edge, too. As they came together, they all but ate each other's mouths, breathing heavily and shaking with the force of the climax.

They ended heaving and gulping air in a sweaty tangle of limbs.

"Sorry, baby. I couldn't wait to get another condom on and I'm not taking any chances with your health."

It took a few seconds for Kitt to have the breath to respond. "No worries. That was intense."

"Yeah, it was," Scott agreed before sliding out of bed again.

Scott returned moments later with another wet washcloth in hand that he used to gently wipe away the remnants of their latest bout of sex. The rough cotton against the still-sensitive skin of his dick made him shudder. A small amount of cum leaked out of the tip, and Scott used his thumb to remove it. That small touch made his balls tingle and his cock tried to rally for a third time, but he was spent. He took in a deep breath, stretched, then settled deeper into the mattress.

When Scott got back into the bed and tucked him once more into his arms, Kitt turned to ask, "Why do that? The cleaning up, I mean?"

Scott shrugged. "I don't know. Habit, I guess. When I was a teenager and eager to lose my cherry, I read in some men's magazine that it was a nice thing to do for a woman. They don't like the mess. I've been doing it since the first time."

Kitt wrapped his arm around Scott's chest. "Do women really not like how messy sex is?"

"I have no idea. I've never actually asked any of them. They did seem to appreciate the effort, though. Why? Does it bother you?"

Kitt could practically hear the frown in Scott's question. "No," he was quick to reassure him. "It was really nice. Other than maybe someone with a particular fetish, I don't think anyone likes waking up to dried cum on their skin."

Scott laced his fingers with Kitt's and held them there on his chest. "Good. I want to do this right." They lay silently together for a while longer. "Is it always like this between two men? I mean, women can come multiple times in one go, but I'm not used to just letting my dick loose in quick succession like that."

Kitt freed his hand to find the side of Scott's ass and give it a squeeze. "It can be whatever we want. Slow, fast, lazy, intense… It's all good."

Scott didn't answer right away, then he hugged Kitt suddenly and with enough force to make him squeak. "I want all of that, and for this to be more than just one night. I want to spend a lot of time exploring your body and our relationship."

Kitt's heart skipped a beat at hearing the R word, but knowing how fraught the situation could become, he tamped down his hopes. "I'm not looking for any kind of commitment, Scott. I can accept whatever you're willing to give me."

"*No.*" Scott's harsh tone surprised him but didn't alarm him. "Sorry. You deserve more than a one-night stand or being the lab rat in my sexual experimentation. I don't want you to ever sell yourself short or allow me to do so." He paused a moment and licked his lips. "I want more, too."

Now Kitt's heart threatened to go into full Gene Kelly mode. "We have more than a week before you have to leave, right?" When Scott nodded, Kitt continued, terrified of saying the wrong thing, yet determined to not run from something that could become glorious. "So let's take it a day at a time, see how it goes. A lot of this is new to you, and that's okay. I get it because I've been there myself."

Scott chuckled and rubbed his chin over the top of Kitt's head. "You're absolutely right about that. And I am…unnerved, I suppose is the right word, but determined not to hide from myself anymore."

Those words eased Kitt's mind quite a bit, although he was still going to keep his hope in check. "This must be doubly hard, given the other shit you're dealing with right now."

Scott's chest rose and fell on a stuttered breath. "Yeah… It's hard. Really fucking hard, but if I'm going to do the memories of J.J. and Hassan justice, I have to face the truth."

Kitt didn't say anything. He sort of knew already what Scott had to come to terms with. And it was the man's right to express it the way he wanted. So Kitt waited as patiently as he could for his lover to say more.

"I loved J.J. like a brother. That's not a lie or a rationalization for the intensity of my feelings for him. But it's also true that I was attracted to him. I would never have acted on it because he was definitely straight and I was stupidly determined to convince myself that I was, too. Also, because having a life-long brother like that would have meant far more to me than sexual gratification. The pull toward him was there, though, and denying it doesn't make his death any easier for me."

Now Kitt felt he had to say something. "It's not your fault that he was killed."

Scott squeezed him briefly before saying, "Technically, legally and even morally, you're right. It was the fucking terrorist who was responsible, as well as the assholes pulling the terrorist's strings. But there is a part of me that can't help feeling otherwise." He hesitated before continuing. "I said that I didn't feel guilty over his death. That was a lie, because I do. In the aftermath of the attack, I lost my shit in a pretty noticeable way. My team tried to ignore it and give me space, while my commander assumed my emotional meltdown was survivor's guilt. That's not the reason, though.

"I picked that restaurant that night," he continued with a hitch to his voice. "I wanted to eat there because I knew Hassan was working. I was attracted to him, too. But I couldn't just go seek him out alone. I didn't have the balls to act on how I felt. So, I made it a team event. Having the guys with me gave me the cover I needed, both with respect to others and my cowardly self. If I hadn't suppressed my nature, we wouldn't have been there and maybe J.J. and Hassan would both still be alive."

Kitt twisted in Scott's arms to hug him full on. "You don't know that. It might have come down to opportunity. The terrorist was looking for a target that night and there you were. But isn't it at least equally likely that you'd been targeted before that? Maybe you'd been surveilled for weeks and they just waited for the right moment to strike?"

Scott tugged the rest of him over his body so they lay flush against each other. His legs entwined with Kitt's, leaving him trapped, yet not in a bad way. "You'd be great in military strategy. That's exactly the kind of analysis we did after it happened. We didn't come to any conclusions, though, and I'm not sure it matters. It *feels* as if I made them both vulnerable by being attracted to them…and, well, it's messing with my head.

"I think losing them both is what's tipped me over the edge. In the Teams, we live with the shadow of death every day. J.J. dying was always going to be a punch to the gut, but we keep fighting even with such awful loss. It's what we signed up for, you know? And I've seen so many good civilians like Hassan die unjustly that it's something I've had to accept."

He gave a shudder, then what sounded like a muted sob. "Having the blood of both men literally on my hands at the same time was more than I could stand. In those moments and in the aftermath, I couldn't help hating myself. I know it's not logical, but it's there and it still hurts so damn much."

Scott fell silent, except for harsh and unsteady breathing. Kitt could tell by the way the man shook and the wetness sliding onto his face that Scott was crying. As a typical alpha male, he was trying to hide it. Kitt gave him the illusion of ignorance, simply holding on and letting Scott hold him tight in return. When the man's breath evened out and the tension in him eased, Kitt dared to offer what comfort he could. He'd said the words, so now he used what skills he had to show the man how he felt.

Wiggling past the circle of Scott's arms, he peppered his throat then chest with soft kisses. Scott gave a brief effort to keep him in place before letting go. His arms flopped to his side, and when Kitt lifted his head, he saw that Scott's eyes were closed. Encouraged by the silent permission, Kitt straddled his lover's wide body and bent over to lave first one nipple, then the other. Scott shivered and groaned—more approval. Kitt concentrated his attention between those two points, sucking them even stiffer. He'd bet no one had ever done such a thing to Scott before and wanted to emphasize how pleasurable a man's pecs could be.

The hard cock that rose between them, tickling Kitt's balls, was the perfect barometer of the effect he was having. It was also a reminder that a man as virile and goal-oriented as Scott wasn't going to accept being teased for very long. So, Kitt licked a line down the man's stomach, following the thin treasure trail, until his lips bumped against the wet head of Scott's cock. He wasted no time sucking it inside, using his tongue to stimulate the bundle of nerves underneath and enjoying the way it made Scott's stomach ripple. With a grunt, Scott raised a hand and placed it on Kitt's head. He didn't press with any real force, but the request was clear enough.

Kitt bobbed down farther, taking the long, thick shaft as far as he could without gagging. He worked it more with his tongue and sucked before taking in a big breath and relaxing his throat. He didn't quite manage to choke the whole thing down, but he got close and felt a measure of pride. The way Scott gasped and bucked, gripping Kitt's hair tight enough to make his eyes water, was immensely gratifying. Maybe this was a first for the man, too, a deep blowjob. Kitt worked the muscles of his throat furiously to make his lover come before he had to surface for air. Scott shouted and raised his hips, sending the last inch or two of his dick where Kitt hadn't thought he could fit it. With tears streaming down his cheek, Kitt sucked his man dry.

When it was over, he slumped on top of Scott, gasping for air, yet thrilled at what he'd done. He'd missed this—finding pleasure in making another man come, in being a good lover. His own dick was hard again, but he didn't care about finding his release once more. The night had been perfect just as it was, and with a large yawn, he realized he was ready to sleep. Scott murmured something about returning the favor, but Kitt hushed him and snuggled closer. Now, Scott was falling asleep, his breathing slowing, his muscles relaxed.

Kitt didn't hesitate to follow him, but as his mind shut down, one last thought flashed through it.

I love him.

Chapter Nine

Scott was known for going into dangerous situations with nerves of steel. This morning, however, as he walked upstairs, he felt as if he were heading into a minefield — one that he felt wholly unequipped to navigate without being blown to smithereens. As he proceeded with a tray balanced in his hands, he gave himself a pep talk, feeling like a fool for doing so. And were his palms actually sweaty? Yes. Yes, they were. He had nothing to be worried about. The night with Kitt had been damn near perfect. That boy wasn't going to break his heart. When Scott had last seen him, he'd been curled up sleeping like the proverbial cat, a peaceful smile on his beautiful face.

Still, the worry was there, just as it had been when he'd woken at dawn, too keyed-up for more sleep. Not even a hard run along the beach had calmed his nerves. But he was a SEAL, for God's sake, and tackling problems head on without hesitation was his forte. And while he couldn't work Kitt's level of magic in the kitchen, he had managed to scramble eggs and toast a bagel to an edible degree. That, and a sweet cup of creamy coffee, would no doubt be met with delight. Kitt was that kind of guy, always grateful for acts of kindness and without a vindictive bone in his body — not that he had any reason to be mad. At least Scott hoped he didn't. He had been replaying the night's events in a constant loop in his head since waking, and it had all left him grinning like a fool. If Kitt was unhappy with the experience, Scott would be surprised.

And still his heart drummed triple time as he quietly opened the door to the master bedroom.

Kitt was lying much as he'd left him, except now his eyes fluttered open and he stared straight at Scott. Slowly, he stretched his arms over his head and his lips curled into a shy grin, letting Scott know all was well. He pushed to a sitting position with the sheet modestly covering his lap. But Scott didn't have to see anything to know what lay beneath. The dimness of the previous night hadn't afforded him a clear view, however, and now he found himself craving an opportunity to explore Kitt's body in stark detail. It was liberating knowing that he most likely could. For his entire adult life, he'd avoided paying attention to other men's bodies. Now, he was free to express his interest openly — to himself most of all.

"Is that for me?"

Kitt's quiet question compelled Scott to focus on his face and not his lap. The kid was adorably rumpled, his long hair curtaining much of his face. It wasn't enough to completely hide the fading bruise on one cheek. Scott had almost gotten used to seeing it, and it was easy to miss if he wasn't looking for it. The sight of it now reminded him of how badly Kitt had been treated in his last relationship. Anger rushed in anew. If he hadn't caught himself in time, he would have caused the tray to crack, given the forceful way he gripped it. He wasn't going to mar one of the best mornings of his life with thoughts of vengeance. Kitt didn't deserve to be reminded, either.

"Who else? Breakfast in bed is a small way of showing you my, uh, affection." He'd almost said 'gratitude', but he didn't want Kitt to feel like he'd been a science experiment.

Kitt smiled shyly again and scooted over toward the middle of the bed to give Scott room to sit beside him. Once the tray was settled over the boy's lap, they sat staring at each for a few seconds. Scott sensed that Kitt wanted to ask him something. There was a bit of wariness in those beautiful eyes, as well, and it took Scott a moment to realize why. He'd been too intoxicated with seeing Kitt in the rumpled bed where they'd made love a few times, the scent of it permeating his nostrils and giving his dick all kinds of ideas.

He shook himself out of the spell of it all to reassure his lover. "I'm not freaking out. I didn't when I first woke and I'm not now. I'm not *ever* going to."

Kitt tucked his hair behind his ears before picking up his mug of coffee and taking a sip. It was a pretty obvious stall, but Scott gave him the space because they had to be careful with each other. Their relationship came with baggage that had to be faced, not ignored, but it would take time. "It's perfect," Kitt said, licking his lips. "You remembered how I like it."

Scott couldn't resist putting his hand on Kitt's lower leg. He needed even this simple contact. "I'm always observant of things that matter."

"You're also a quick learner." Kitt stifled a giggle before grabbing his fork and trying the eggs. "You didn't have to bring me breakfast in bed, but I'm glad you did. I'm starving." Scott couldn't help preening a little at that confession. "Don't look so smug," Kitt added with a teasing roll of his eyes.

"I can't help it," Scott confessed with an answering grin. Then he turned sober. "I don't want you to worry that I'm having second thoughts, baby. Last night was liberating. I feel free, not conflicted or horrified or any of the other awful scenarios that you might be worried about. With good reason," he was quick to add. "Coming out of the closet—even the bisexual one—is hard, and I bet you figure a guy like me might be inclined to fight it, even after a night like we had. Maybe more so, given how amazing it was."

Kitt swallowed his mouthful of food and chased it with more coffee before answering. "I woke earlier and found you'd gone." His gaze dropped. "I confess I had a tough moment thinking you'd run screaming silently from my side and were figuring out how to dismiss what we'd shared as an aberration or a mistake." He lifted his eyes to stare at Scott again and the affection shining through them was unmistakable. "Then, a second later, I realized that you're not that kind of guy. You weren't going to blame alcohol or me for something you did. You're an honorable man. So I went back to sleep, convinced that I had nothing to worry about. Although," he added with a grimace, "I'll understand if you want to keep it to just the one night."

Scott slid his hand to cup Kitt's inner thigh. "I haven't changed my mind, Kitt. We have time to get to know each other better. I *want* to do that, to spend more time with you, in bed and out of it. In fact, it's a beautiful day. We should do something fun outdoors."

The tension eased from Kitt even before he responded. "I'd like that." The boy kept eating, and the way he devoured the simple meal made Scott feel like a domestic goddess. "Did you have anything in mind? I love hanging out on the beach."

With any doubts eased, Scott got excited with thoughts of the day. "Yeah, that's certainly part of the plan, but I was thinking we could go kayaking. I know a great spot where we can rent them and paddle along a tidal estuary."

"I've never been," Kitt said with his mouth half full. "But I can swim pretty well, so I'm game."

Scott couldn't help rubbing his lover's leg as he spoke. "We'll wear lifejackets, plus I'm a SEAL, remember? I won't let you drown, no matter what."

Kitt fluttered his eyelashes. "Good. And I trust you."

The simple declaration caused Scott's chest to puff. "I'm glad to hear that." He slid his fingers to a spot just beneath Kitt's balls. They were tight, and that could only mean one thing. His own cock swelled in response. "After you eat, we should take a shower…together."

Kitt's eyes widened. "Your hair's wet. You've already done that."

Scott shrugged as if it were no big deal, when his whole body was humming at the thought of getting a naked Kitt into the bathroom. "A quick rinse outside. I need someone to soap me all over, while I do the same to him."

Kitt stared at him with dilated pupils for a few seconds before lifting the tray off his lap. "All done."

He practically dropped it back on the bed and forced Scott to move so that he could throw the sheet off.

Scott grunted as if being sucker-punched in the gut at the sight of a naked and aroused Kitt. He had no trouble appreciating the man's beauty. In that second, he couldn't imagine a time when desiring another man had been taboo for him. Without thinking, he reached for Kitt and hoisted him by his hips for a kiss. The boy responded by throwing his arms around his neck and wrapping his legs around Scott's waist. Their hard cocks mashed together as they devoured each other's mouths. Scott carried Kitt into the bathroom and fiddled with the shower without letting their lips separate. It was only once the temperature was right that he eased Kitt down and stripped off his own clothing.

He was no stranger to shower sex and had always preferred it to be as easy and natural as possible. That meant no penetration, so no condoms or awkward poses. He used his hand, as always. This time, however, he was able to please himself and his lover at once. It was easy having sex with another man. All he had to do was repeat what he'd done in bed, grabbing both shafts and jerking them together. He pressed Kitt against the wall as he did so, thrusting his tongue inside his mouth, keeping a firm grip on him with his other arm.

Kitt heaved and bucked into his hold, yet also managed to cup Scott's ass with one hand and dig his nails into his skin. That bite of pain was surprisingly delicious. It was enough to send him over the edge, his orgasm crashing into him with such force that he had to work at staying upright. Kitt came too, their cum spilling over Scott's fingers, mingling in a way that made him feel a primal sense of possessiveness. For a few seconds, he wanted to hold on to Kitt and never let him go. The force of the impulse almost frightened him, but it eased. He let go, then broke the kiss. They stood pressed together as their breathing evened out.

"Wow," Kitt finally said, chuckling into Scott's chest. "You make me come so hard."

Again, that sense of pride hit him. "Yeah, and you're helping me set some kind of record for a man of my age."

Kitt playfully swatted him. "You're not that old."

"In SEAL years I am." Because he didn't want to think about how he was only on leave for several more days, Scott put aside the conversation and steered Kitt under the spray. "Let me wash you."

"Hmm."

Kitt's almost purr of agreement sent a spark to Scott's dick. It jerked as if to rise again before giving in to the reality of biology. That was fine with him. He wanted no distractions while he lathered soap over Kitt's lovely body. Under the bright light of the bathroom, he had a clear view of every inch he touched. It was both familiar and not. On the surface, Kitt had the same things as Scott, but the differences were there to see as well. His lover's body was slender, yet toned, and wholly masculine.

It wasn't as if Kitt were feminine, just a more refined version of Scott's own body. The lack of breasts didn't bother him, even though it was one of the features of a woman that most fascinated him. Kitt's pecs weren't better or worse than what a woman had to offer, merely different. The fact that he could hold a cock instead of dipping his fingers into the soft folds of a vulva intrigued him. It was a different kind of fun exploration. He realized with an instant of clarity that he was a lucky bastard to be able to feast from both sides of the table. He almost pitied those who were more limited.

When he turned Kitt to wash his back, he lingered over the guy's small, taut ass. It was the perfect handful for him—and smooth, like most of Kitt's skin. He trailed his fingers through the soap all over the globes before dipping one down the crack between them. He circled the puckered hole with tentative swirls, worried that he would hurt the boy. Kitt's moan and the way he leaned into Scott alleviated his concerns. He pressed his fingertip inside. The sphincter tightened around him, a sign of his welcome.

"Are you sore?"

Kitt shook his head. "No more than usual after being well-fucked." He squeezed Scott's finger before relaxing again. "I like it because it reminds me of your being inside me."

Because it was too tempting to try to go another round, Scott pulled his finger out and proceeded to rinse the soap off Kitt. Then he washed the boy's hair, loving the feel of the strands slipping through his fingers. This was something very familiar. He'd done it for women plenty of times. When it was finished, he tried to make quick work of his own shampoo and second shower of the day. Kitt wouldn't let him, though, lathering his hands and running them all over Scott's body, much as he'd done to him. Those clever hands lingered on his dick, which once more tried to rally. It was half-hearted at best.

Kitt giggled. "Sorry. Didn't mean to tax you, old man. Maybe later." He fluttered those long lashes again.

Scott kissed him hard before saying, "Count on it."

* * * *

Kitt had rested the paddle across his lap and just sat there taking in the view. Although Scott couldn't see his face, he could tell by the set of the guy's shoulders that his lover was relaxed and enjoying himself.

It was the perfect day for water sports, and Scott surveyed the peaceful setting. A person couldn't be a SEAL if they were afraid of heights or small places or couldn't stand being food for bugs. Jumping out of planes, crawling inside shafts and pipes and lying for hours in a swamp was all part of the job. And they had to be someone who never, ever gave up. But to Scott's way of thinking, one of the most essential requirements for being a member of the elite force was that the person really had to *love* water. It was kind of built into the name, after all.

In that regard, he was perfect for his job. Being here in this amazing setting with someone he cared about was heaven on Earth. No knock on the interior states — there was beauty and majesty there, too — but he couldn't imagine not returning to live by the sea. This was where he belonged. He didn't feel the need to press on, to tire himself out with exercise. His emotional state was better than it had been since returning home from that awful deployment. It was utter contentedness, an emotional healing that was achieved by more than simply the setting. The view of Kitt's back was on par with the still water, the bright green marshy land and the haunting calls of birds. *Delightful, soothing.*

"This is so wonderful!" Kitt turned his head to look at Scott over his shoulder. His face was lit up with innocent glee.

Something inside Scott burst. It was another one of those sucker-punch reactions, except this time, he had no trouble identifying the location of it or its meaning. It was love, pure and simple. It squeezed his heart and made it hard to breathe. He actually put a fist to it and rubbed, as if that would somehow change how he felt. In the next instant, he stopped and relaxed into the reaction. It wasn't so scary. Maybe it wasn't even real, only a form of gratitude for Kitt unlocking what had been inside him all along. Kitt's smile started to falter. He'd seen Scott's initial reaction without knowing the whole of it.

Scott grinned broadly, wanting to alleviate any worry. "It is. It's perfect. But let's head back. I'm starving. Want to get some subs from the Quick Mart for lunch?"

"Yes, please! And we should get something for dinner. I know we've already bought a lot, but I have a taste for grilled chicken. I have this great teriyaki marinade recipe, if that's okay."

"Perfect." As he started paddling again, Scott envisioned how the rest of the day would play out, including what the night would bring.

* * * *

His cock was spent. There was no way Scott could go another round with his lover, no matter how much he wanted to. Kitt, on the other hand, had the resilience of most men his age. He was already hard again from Scott's soft caresses. He hadn't meant for the touch to be erotic. It was simply that he couldn't get enough physical contact with this boy. The whole day he'd found himself touching what he could when Kitt was nearby. It wasn't all sexual. Running his fingers along Kitt's arm or sliding them through the boy's silky hair was just as satisfying. *Well, almost as much.* He hugged him closer and inhaled his scent. It was more than the shampoo he'd used in the morning. There was something else that he now recognized as uniquely Kitt. And if that sounded like some cheesy line from a romance novel, tough shit. He understood now that it was real and true. For the first time in his life, he was connected to someone with all his senses.

Gratifyingly, Kitt snuggled closer. One of his small hands clasped Scott's limp cock. "Have I worn you out?"

Scott chuckled. "You have to ask? I've lost count of how many times I've come in the last twenty-four hours." There had been more lovemaking after lunch, as well as in the evening.

"Hmm. Me too." Kitt grabbed his hip and pressed closer. "I can't tell you how grateful I am that you've given this back to me."

Scott frowned. "What?"

"My sexuality. I'd buried it for so long because it had become tied to fear of Emilio's abuse. Nothing seemed to satisfy him, no matter how hard I tried, so I gave up. Sex became a chore without pleasure, not that he cared one way or the other about how I felt. I thought I might have lost the ability to enjoy sex forever. You gave it back to me."

A spurt of fury almost consumed Scott. Domestic abuse had always appalled him, especially when he saw it on deployment, because some men in those countries didn't bother to hide it. Never before had he faced it in such a personal way, however. Even though he had no idea what this Emilio fucker looked like, he still pictured smashing a fist into his nose. He tamped down his reaction. Kitt didn't need that right at the moment, so much as reassurance. "You took it back, babe. That's how strong you are."

"Am I? Strong, I mean. Here and now, I feel as if I am. But that's because of the confidence you've given me. Only a week ago, I would have disputed it." His chest rose and fell on a quick breath. "It took so long for me to break free from that violence. At first it was because I was so sure Emilio's outbursts were my fault."

"Never!" Scott couldn't help the vehement denial. "Abuse is *never* the victim's fault."

"My brain knew that, but it was overridden by my emotions and experiences. Before I left, my family had spent years telling me that I was damaged, worthless…evil. It was hard to keep fighting against that view, to maintain a sense of value and rightness.

"Once I was on my own, my experiences didn't change my perception of myself very much. The men I met and hooked up with liked me just fine for sex, and that was all. I still couldn't see my value beyond my body being a source of pleasure. Emilio was the first man to treat me like a person and not a convenient place to stick his dick."

"Oh, baby." Scott tried to keep a tender hold on his lover when all he still wanted to do was smash his fist into something. Someone. *All of them.* He knew, though, that not all battles were fought that way. Kitt needed a safe place to vent more than anything else, much as

Scott had earlier. Hard as it was, he bit his tongue and just listened.

"It wasn't all bad, better than it had been at home." Kitt went silent for a while. "Emilio got me off the streets and helped me get my hairdressing degree. That was a huge, positive step in my life. I hadn't realized it at the time, but it was his way of making extra money for himself off my labor.

"Anyway, when Emilio started being abusive, it was easy to believe him when he said it was my fault. I tried really hard to please him. Eventually, I understood that there was nothing I could do. He was always going to find fault, no matter what. After that, I was simply terrified of what would happen if I tried to leave him. I became stuck in this cycle that I couldn't break free from. He controlled every aspect of my life, including my friends. If not for Karen giving me a safe haven, I wouldn't have had the guts to leave."

Scott kissed the top of Kitt's head, a gentle reminder that he was still safe and valued. "I get the fear and the despair. I've seen a lot of people living with it so much that they couldn't help me and my team protect them against their enemies. When someone stronger than you exerts their power long enough, it's hard to see that they can be defeated, that they're not invincible. We had to work long and hard to build up trust."

"It's obvious to me now that it was a toxic relationship and that I deserve better," Kitt said. His voice hitched when he added, "All I want is someone kind and decent who loves me, who will build a life with me. Have kids, maybe." He paused. "Yeah, I'd really like to have a marriage and children with a house of our own, a minivan for me and some flashier car for my husband that he spends time washing and waxing on weekends, and…a dog running around the backyard." He giggled. "Pretty basic stuff, right? My friends, such as they are, would roll their eyes at how bougie my dreams sound."

Scott disagreed with all those assholes who hadn't stood behind Kitt when he'd needed them. What Kitt described sounded pretty damn perfect to him, even though he hadn't entertained that vision of a future for himself before. "If that's another way of saying awesome, I agree." He cupped Kitt's perfect ass and added, "Don't let anyone tell you your dreams fall short of some ideal they have in their heads. What you want sounds fantastic and we're lucky to be living in a time and place where they are easily within reach."

Kitt bucked his hips, brushing his erection against Scott's still-exhausted groin. "I just need to find a husband. Easier said than done."

Me. Scott almost blurted that out loud. The urge was strong, yet he stifled it. Things between him and Kitt had already progressed at warp speed. It was too soon for him to make that kind of commitment. Instead, he said, "You're so young. You've got plenty of time."

"True." He snuggled some more, a gesture that sent Scott's heart skipping a beat in its simple affection. "It's scary, though, to think of loving someone enough to marry them and also risk losing them to all kinds of things — death, divorce."

"You can't think like that — otherwise, life will pass you by. You live in the moment, focus on the quarter you're playing, to use a football analogy, and not on the next one."

"I suppose that's critical for being a SEAL."

"It is. That and never giving up."

"Are a lot of SEALs married?"

"Sure, about the same amount as you'd find in any population. And they're parents, too." Like most Teams, his was tight-knit and socialized a lot. Their families had formed their own community to support each other when their husbands and fathers were on deployment. He hadn't given it much thought, but now that he did, he realized that would be important to him, knowing his own family would have that kind of emotional and physical help while he was out of the country and unable to do anything for them. But his very next thought was whether a husband of his would be welcome in the same way — or would he always be on the outside? Okay, now he was doing what he'd advised Kitt not to — fretting over the fourth quarter when he hadn't finished the first one.

"It must be so hard for their families when they're deployed. How do they cope with the fear? It's not like kissing your husband goodbye, then seeing him drive off into commuter traffic. I mean, the roads can be dangerous, but it's not like they're getting shot at or bombed routinely." A shudder ran through him.

A frisson of alarm sprinted through Scott's nervous system at the observation, for reasons that he wasn't willing to face at that moment. "Yeah, military families are a special breed for sure. That's doubly true for those in special operations. Our families know that whenever we deploy, we're in the thick of it. That's what we do, run toward the danger. I won't lie... Some can't hack it. Divorce is a real problem."

"I don't know if I would ever have that kind of strength. Not that it's an issue for me or anything," Kitt quickly added.

And Scott understood why. This conversation was picking up speed and going in a direction that neither of them was ready to head toward. Their relationship, if it could be called one instead of a fling, was only a minute old. Kitt was still suffering the effects of an abusive partner, and Scott had to admit that he would still struggle somewhat to get comfortable with his newly acknowledged identity outside the beach house. Despite trying not to think about it, he was having a hard time picturing how a same-sex couple fit into the SEAL community—into his own team's social fabric. Would his teammates be accepting of him? The rules would force them to not say or do anything overt, yet nothing compelled them to welcome the situation socially with open arms. It wasn't really himself that he'd worry about. Kitt deserved to be treated with warmth and respect. Scott wouldn't want to shove him into an environment that shunned him, to leave him isolated when he'd need others the most. Spouses relied on the support of the community when the team was deployed.

And, once again, he was getting way ahead of the situation. All this worry was purely hypothetical.

It was time to switch gears and deal with the more immediate problem of Kitt's continued arousal. They both needed sleep, and while he gave it one more try to rally his own cock, there was nothing doing. Only getting Kitt off would be easy. All he had to do was clasp the shaft and give it few tugs to make the boy come. He knew Kitt's sweet body almost as well as his own, even after such a short time. Kitt deserved more attention than that, though. So far, their physical relationship had been too one-sided, by Scott's way of thinking. It was time to even it out. Besides, if Scott were serious about fully exploring his sexuality with another man, he needed to test the boundaries of what he could handle.

Mind made up, he rolled Kitt onto his back without warning and claimed his mouth in a heated kiss. When they were both in need of air, he pulled back and said, "Let me help you relax to get to sleep."

Kitt moaned and bucked into him. "That would be lovely, thanks."

Using his lips to lay down a trail of quick, wet kisses, Scott straddled Kitt's legs. It was easy to employ the same technique he'd mastered with women's breasts to the boy's nipples. He'd been surprised at how much of an erogenous zone his own had been when Kitt had done the same to him. He proceeded to nip and suck, swirling his tongue around the hard nubs, delighting in the way that Kitt shuddered and moaned. Scott continued the journey downward, stopping to explore the bling around Kitt's navel. Was this an area of pleasure, too? Probably not, but Kitt's flat stomach rippled nevertheless when Scott teased the metal ring with his tongue.

But when Scott flicked his tongue on the tip of Kitt's cock, his eyes flew open. He stared at him and started to lift his head. "What...?"

Scott gently pressed the heel of one palm against Kitt's forehead to stop the motion. "Lie still, baby, and enjoy."

"You don't have—"

"I want to." He made his tone playful in order to mask the slight freak-out he was having inside his head. So far, everything he'd done with Kitt was not so different from his experiences with a woman. Giving his male lover a blowjob was an essential test of his true attraction. No way he was going to let this, or any other relationship with another man, be all about his pleasure and his comfort zone. Sex was a two-way street, each party obligated to at least try to meet the other's needs. *The same goes for love.* That thought was a bridge too far for him at the moment, so he pushed it aside and concentrated on Kitt's erection.

That first tentative lick had been benign, a testing of the waters. Bending over again, he ran his tongue up the entire shaft from base to head, swirling around the slit. Now, he tasted the combination of bitter and salt that he expected. In the early discovery of masturbation, he'd tried his own cum out of curiosity. It had only been the one time, but now the memory came flooding back with Kitt's pre-cum reminding his taste buds. It wasn't unpleasant, and the way Kitt moaned from the touch egged Scott to go full bore. His lover deserved this devoted attention, and Scott was willing to bet it had been a while since anyone had bothered to pleasure him this way. But those thoughts made him think of Emilio, the fucker, and he didn't want that asshole in bed with them.

Blotting all thoughts from his mind, he put his full attention into his first blowjob. It wasn't that hard. He knew what he liked and just went with that. He spent a few seconds lavishing Kitt's cock with his tongue before returning to the tip and wrapping his lips around the head entirely. Kitt gasped and bucked instantly, sending the shaft farther down Scott's throat. He clamped his lips tightly and held it in place, wanting some time to adjust to the novel experience. The hard, hot dick lay heavy on his tongue. The skin was satiny smooth. He worked his tongue around it and sucked, taking it in a little bit farther.

Kitt whimpered and wiggled his hips in an obvious plea for more. Kitt had thrown his head back against the mattress and his chin quivered. He fisted the sheets with a white-knuckled grip. Scott reached for both hands to clasp them and entwined their fingers. Now he could feel the tension in his boy. He was close to coming. *So very close.* Making that happen became Scott's mission. Reluctantly, he closed his eyes and, with a deep breath, plunged his mouth down to brush against Kitt's pubic mound. The dick slid into his throat, almost making him gag. He swallowed convulsively to massage the shaft. He kept on doing so as Kitt shouted and writhed and didn't stop until his lover went boneless.

Scott made sure to keep running his tongue along the shaft to taste every drop of cum that was left. He didn't want to cheat either of them out of the full experience. A few more shudders ran through Kitt before he was completely still. By the time Scott had returned to the boy's side, Kitt's breath had started to even out. He murmured something unintelligible as Scott gathered him close, before going silent again. As Scott covered them both with a sheet and settled himself, he knew that he'd still been fighting against a rising tide. It didn't matter that everything was happening so quickly. If he spent the next ten years living in this cozy cottage with Kitt, it wasn't going to change a thing.

He loved Kitt. So what was he going to do about it? There was only one possible answer. Plan the mission, then tackle and complete it. Failure was not an option. All he had to do was accept that and figure out a way to convince Kitt that Scott was worthy of his love and that being married to a SEAL was something Kitt could handle.

And if I can't, would Scott leave the Teams for me? He didn't know and it wasn't something he could face at the moment, nor did he need to. He was looking at that blasted fourth quarter again. He had days to figure it out, and not alone. Kitt was the other half of the equation and Scott wasn't going to disrespect him by making assumptions or denying him a say in how they proceeded. They would talk and figure it out together. That was what couples did. And with that firm plan in his head, he let sleep claim him.

Chapter Ten

Kitt spritzed a brisk cologne on Scott's smooth cheeks as the cap to the shave. Unlike before, this time, he could run his fingers along the skin with a lingering devotion to catch any stray stubble that he might have missed. He could even press a quick kiss to those upturned lips, except that Scott wasn't going to let him get away with the brevity. Before Kitt could pull away, the guy took him by the arms and tumbled him onto his lap. Then it was all about long and lingering, leaving him breathless and almost giddy with happiness. These last couple of days with Scott had been everything he'd dreamed of in life.

He had to work at tamping down his joy. This relationship was too new and sudden to use as a basis for happily ever after. Given that Scott's sexuality was, as yet, in the exploration stage and Kitt's own lingering trauma from Emilio, it would be particularly crazy to just jump into something permanent.

Here, in this cottage by the sea, everything was perfect. They lived in their own bubble. It was easy for both of them to forget that the outside world existed. But was it really possible for Scott to return to his macho, traditionally homophobic job with a boyfriend in tow? Although the man didn't lack courage, to put it mildly, revealing one's sexual identity might be harder than facing bullets and bombs. When he was fighting, it was the enemy he faced. With his personal life, he'd be squaring off against his friends. Kitt knew all too well what it felt like when friends and family turned their backs on a person.

In Scott's case, he depended on these men to stay alive.

For his own part, he wasn't sure he was cut out for that kind of life, either. It had to be terribly hard to see a loved-one head out to certain, horrible danger and get on with a daily routine while waiting for someone to drive up and announce that he was dead. He wasn't sure he had that kind courage himself. And he wasn't convinced that all the support among SEAL families Scott had told him about would be available to him. Maybe he was doing them all a disservice, but he'd been shunned by those he'd trusted and liked, loved even, before. He wasn't a naïve teenager now, thinking that the world had changed enough that he could be accepted for who he was by everyone.

He told himself it was too soon to fret over these things, but the thoughts always returned. There wasn't much time left for them to figure out at least the basics. He tried to follow Scott's advice to live in the moment. To that end, he swatted his man playfully and slid to his feet. "Stop. I've got work to do. The laundry is piling up and we're out of almost everything. Clean sheets in particular are at a premium at this point." He gave Scott a knowing look. "We need to go food shopping, too.

How can one man each so much?" He popped his eyes in mock consternation.

Scott gave him a lazy smile as he stood and stretched. *Jesus, the way that man fills a T-shirt is sinful.* "If we split the chores, we'll get them done in half the time. We can use what's left of the day for other, more entertaining things." Butter wouldn't melt in his mouth as he said those words, yet their meaning was clear.

Kitt's whole body reacted with a delightful spark of arousal. It would be so easy to just forget everything else and head back upstairs. Or maybe they wouldn't make it past the kitchen. There were plenty of surfaces to sit on or lean over, and the sweet ache he felt after so many penetrations wasn't a deterrent, either. He knew the difference between pleasure and pain, and what Scott gave him was squarely in the former category. Plus, he knew with a certainty that eased all fears that if he told Scott to stop, he would. If he asked him to change course during lovemaking, the man would…and had.

He shook his head. Someone had to be sensible. "Work first, Lieutenant Carpenter. Pleasure later, and it will be all the better for having been well-earned."

Scott rolled his eyes. "You sound like Grammy." He swooped down to claim another soul-sucking kiss before going inside. "I'll leave right now and get the food. Sorry if I'm being boringly repetitive, but I'm going to get the *sub* for myself again." He grabbed his keys from the counter. "What would you like?"

Kitt gathered his shaving kit and stepped across the threshold of the sliding doors. "As if I didn't know that already, and I'll take the same, thanks. Oh, and strawberries and rhubarb. I want to make a pie."

"You got it, babe." Scott paused on his way to the front door and stared at Kitt for a few seconds. It seemed as if he wanted to say more. Then he flashed a smile and was gone.

Kitt's heartbeat increased as if something important had happened, even though it hadn't. Not on Scott's part, anyway. But he knew what was happening for him, what had happened already a couple of days ago. He'd fallen in love with Scott. All his thoughts about reclaiming his life and fretting over how he'd fit into Scott's world were just so much background noise. The important truth was there, front and center, if he dared to look at it. Another week with this man wasn't going to be enough. He wanted more, desperately. And it didn't matter how much sense it made or whether a future with Scott was what was best for either of them. His heart knew what it wanted, and his brain could go to hell.

With his mood threatening to spiral downward, he shook off the thoughts once again. He needed to focus on the here and now, and that meant getting the dough made for the pie crust and into the fridge for chilling. He pulled the screen door shut and latched it but didn't bother with the glass one. There was a nice breeze coming onshore and it would cool the house a little without artificial help. Plus, the smell of the ocean, as well as the sounds of it, always soothed his nerves. He cleaned his shaving implements carefully, as always, before putting them away and throwing in a load of laundry. There was something extra lovely about mixing his clothing now with Scott's. Then he pulled out the food processor and got to work.

* * * *

Scott drove to the center of town with the windows down. It was too nice a day for air conditioning. He found himself whistling, too, being in an almost disgustingly cheery mood. It wasn't really his style, at least not historically. Lately, since he'd been making love non-stop to another man—no, specifically with *Kitt*—his demeanor had changed. It wasn't merely that the weight of J.J.'s and Hassan's deaths had started to ease. His whole outlook had changed. He'd even started to think positively in terms of something that had always been a source of distress for him—what his life would be like once he could no longer deploy as a SEAL. That eventuality had always appeared pretty grim in his mind. Now, he saw the possibility of having a new and equally wonderful life, one that involved having a family.

Having Kitt. Because really, that was where his mind was turning—had turned in the last couple of days. Being with this one man had become more than just an exploration of his sexuality. He wanted more than Kitt's body. He enjoyed more. Kitt was wonderful, a resilient person who, for all that he'd been through, was essentially optimistic. He made Scott happy simply by smiling at him, especially after they'd made love and Kitt's expression told Scott that he'd done the job well. He'd helped Kitt with his healing just as Kitt had helped him with his. They seemed tailor-made for each other…if not for that one thing.

"No, it's only a thing if you make it one, jackass." Scott gripped the steering wheel hard, disgusted with himself for having doubts. His teammates had never let him down before, and there was no reason to assume they would now. His own team hadn't been among those operators who spoke disparagingly behind their hands about the out, gay SEAL, at least not around him. They would accept him as he was, and their wives would take Kitt under their protective wings as a new member of their community.

He had to have faith in these people. They were good and caring. It might take some time for them to adjust, but they would. Neither would he be the last SEAL to come out. Others would follow, probably more than anyone expected, and women were entering the Teams, as well. Soon it would become boringly familiar for Team families to include husbands.

"Holy shit, am I talking myself into marriage?" He laughed as he hunted for a parking space near the market.

And he worked it all out in his mind because that was what he did. Kitt could easily move out to California, given that he had no lease to get out of and had everything he owned with him already. There was no furniture to ship across the country or job to give notice to. Scott could support him while Kitt did whatever he needed to become a licensed hairdresser in his new state. The logistics of what he was planning wouldn't be that hard.

By the time he spotted a space about to be vacated, he had it all figured out and nearly slammed on his brakes as the arrogance of it all hit him square in the face. Kitt was not a mission to be planned or a problem to solve. He was an independent human being who had just escaped from a relationship with a man who'd controlled him. Scott's good intentions notwithstanding, he had no more right than that asshole, Emilio, to make decisions for the boy. If Scott really wanted to be a strong man, he'd lay his heart out on the table in front of Kitt and either take a licking if his lover didn't feel the same way, or they'd work out their future together. Now, *that* was a plan.

As he waited for the other driver to ease out of the space, his phone rang. Seeing who was calling, he answered with a cheery, "Hey."

"Hi, where are you?"

Something in Karen's tone had him on high alert within seconds. "What's wrong?"

"Nothing...probably."

"Come on, Karen. I'm alone in the SUV in the center of town. Kitt's back at the cottage, so speak to me."

"Okay, this may be my overactive imagination, but I just got in this morning because I had a meeting off site, and I think someone's been messing with my stuff. We do have a new overnight cleaning service at the office, so maybe it was just sloppiness."

"What stuff?" Scott didn't move even though the space was clear now.

"That's what's making me uncomfortable. You know that picture we took right before Grandpa died, the one where we're all standing in front of the cottage's door? The one that I have in a cheesy tourist frame that has the name of the town on it?"

Unease crept in and he was already getting ready to hang a u-turn. "Karen, cut to the chase."

"I keep it on the top shelf of my bookcase, but I found it lower down, as if someone had picked it up and looked at it before replacing it wrong."

Scott's tires squealed as he turned the SUV around to head back the way he'd come. "Call Kitt. Tell him to stay inside with the doors locked." Frustration bubbled up because he couldn't warn his lover himself. In all the time they'd been together, he still hadn't bothered to get Kitt's number. It hadn't been necessary.

"It could be nothing."

"You don't believe that. I assume Emilio knew about your friendship with Kitt?"

"Yes, he did," came the biting reply, laced with fear. "We met once, and I couldn't hide my anger at him, I'm sorry to say."

"Right, so it's not absurd for him to think Kitt ran to you for help. What better way for that fucker to track him down than gain access to your office through some cleaning company? Call Kitt and scare the crap out of him — whatever it takes to keep him safe. Believe me… If this is all unnecessary panic, I'll go to bed a happy man tonight."

"Right. Calling now. Be careful, Scott." She hung up without a goodbye.

Tossing his phone on the passenger seat, Scott gripped the wheel with both hands and floored it. The speed limit be dammed.

* * * *

Kitt put the dough into the refrigerator to chill. He'd made a double batch because he'd neglected to tell Scott how much fruit to buy. Knowing his lover's gargantuan appetite, he'd likely buy enough for two pies. That was fine. It wouldn't go to waste and he did so love seeing Scott enjoy his cooking. A cracking sound had him whirling around. He knew even before he saw Emilio lunging past the broken screen door that it wasn't Scott coming back sooner than expected.

He stifled the instant of panic as well as the whimper that threatened to pop out of his mouth. The time for cringing and showing fear to this violent bully was over. He needed to be strong because, for a certainty,

Scott would be back soon and make Emilio sorry he'd tracked him down. In the meantime, he was on his own, and Scott had shown him that he was stronger than he'd believed himself to be.

"Here you are," Emilio said in the oozing tone that was part mocking and part chastisement, as if Kitt were a wayward pet or something. "I've been so worried since you disappeared, but of course, I knew that bitch had something to do with it, so it was only a matter of time before I had a chance to find out where she'd hidden you. I had to pretend to clean toilets for an entire night. That's how devoted I've been."

Kitt straightened his shoulders. "What are you doing here? I won't go back with you."

Emilio's face fell in a moment of almost sadness. "I know that. You're too stupid to understand how good it was between us. Although," he added with a sudden snarl, "given the shit-eating grin on your new daddy's face as he left, you must have improved on your fucking skills."

Ignoring the insult to both himself and Scott, Kitt put as much force as he could muster into his voice. "Get out, Emilio. Seriously, you don't want to be here when he returns." He took a step back when Emilio moved toward him, knowing there was no route he could take to any of the exits that would allow him to escape. The man was bigger, faster and stronger than Kitt and would be able to block and contain him before he managed to leave the house. If by some miracle Kitt got outside, he'd still be quickly caught. He held out no hope that screaming would be heard by anyone. The houses weren't that close together at this end of the beach.

Emilio's expression telegraphed how well he understood that Kitt was cornered. Worse, breaking into the cottage had been a significant escalation, as had his efforts to locate Kitt. Abuse toward Kitt had morphed into criminal activity against others, too. He'd been worried in the end that Emilio was mentally unstable. The way the guy's eyes were shining brightly, he knew he'd been right. There would no reasoning with him. It was a matter of holding the monster at bay until Scott came to the rescue.

The ringing of his phone, which he'd left at the far end of his counter, distracted them both. Kitt knew it had to be Karen. Who else? When he didn't pick up, he hoped she'd call Scott. No, he *knew* she would, because Karen was a worrier and a doer. If she thought there was a problem, she'd act on solving it. Unfortunately, there was no more a way for him to reach his phone before Emilio than for him to reach the exits. Kitt needed to level the playing field as it currently existed. He might be cornered, but he wasn't helpless. His short time with Scott had given him a renewed sense of self-worth and inherent courage. Emilio's fleeting focus on the phone gave him a chance to move farther into the kitchen area. He grabbed a knife out of the block sitting on the counter and pointed it in Emilio's direction.

"Get. Out." He was proud of how steady his voice was, even while his heart felt as if it scrambled around his chest like a hamster on a wheel.

Emilio almost looked pleased. His face split in a broad, bone-chilling smile. "Someone's under the delusion that he's grown some balls."

Now the man advanced on Kitt with a steady gait, his gaze never leaving Kitt's. He grabbed a dishtowel from the oven door handle without hitching a step and wrapped it around his left arm. With nowhere to go, Kitt had no choice but to lash out once he was in range, trying to cut his attacker somewhere vulnerable, even as Emilio raised his left arm in defense. Too late, he realized he should have tried stabbing with his left hand into Emilio's open right side. Kitt cried out in frustration as his former lover easily disarmed him.

Wrapping Kitt's hair into his left fist, Emilio pulled him in close and held the knife to his neck. "Stupid bitch. Did you really think you could best me? Did you really think you could *leave* me? Ingrate! You owe me. Don't forget I made you, trained you, and I didn't do it so you could slut around in other men's beds."

Kitt didn't bother to argue. There had been a time when he'd believed all that because he hadn't valued himself enough. *No more.* Talking was a waste of time. He put all his strength into resisting as much as he could as Emilio pulled him over to the screen door he'd wrecked, leading out to the back deck. Kitt only had a second to register his surprise. He knew Emilio must have parked his car somewhere on the road. While he hadn't heard a car entering the driveway, the front door was still the shortest route to the road. Why wasn't the man pulling him out of that door?

It hardly mattered. Emilio had the strength to literally drag him by his hair. The upside was that while the man kept hold of the knife, he was no longer bothering to try to press it against any part of Kitt's body. The burning heat of the deck on his bare soles gave him a chance to honestly try to slow their progress, except Emilio first ignored then dismissed his pleas to go back for his shoes.

"You won't need them," was his dismissive reply.

Kitt grabbed the hand holding him and tried to dig his nails into Emilio's flesh. He might as well have been gouging stone for all the good it did. "What's the plan, Emilio? You know I won't go back to our old life. This is crazy," he added, knowing that was going to earn him a slap.

Emilio surprised him by laughing. "You stupid boy. I warned you what would happen if you tried to leave me."

No trying, asshole. I did *leave you.* He wanted to shout his response, but he needed every breath to keep from falling as he was forced down the stairs and onto the beach. The sand wasn't any better than the wood. He hissed with pain and almost felt relief when Emilio tugged him toward the cool, wet stretch at the water's edge — until he realized with a heart-stopping jolt what that meant.

He tried to dig in his heels, ignoring the sting of his hair being tightly pulled. "No! I'm not going to let you do this." Emilio merely laughed again as they both waded into the fringes of the surf. "You can't want to spend the rest of your life in jail. They'll know it was you." He didn't even care about the mounting panic in his tone.

Emilio stopped abruptly and turned, causing Kitt to bump into his chest. He hauled Kitt onto his toes and pressed their faces together. His hot breath caused Kitt to flinch. He couldn't understand how he'd ever thought this man worthy of his love. "I'm not the stupid one. We go together."

Kitt blinked wildly as the importance of those words sank in. Once they did, he struggled like a madman, no longer concerned with the knife being used against him, not when Emilio intended to drown them both in the frigid ocean. His efforts didn't stop Emilio from continuing into the water, and Kitt couldn't hold back a sob as his fear rocketed.

A shout penetrated his fog of desperation. When he twisted his head to look, the sight of Scott racing toward them gave him the final spurt of strength he needed. He scratched Emilio's face, drawing blood, a sight that gave him grim satisfaction. It was enough to cause the man's grip to loosen a bit. With a violent tug, Kitt freed himself and stumbled back.

He managed to stay on his feet and turned to flee away from Emilio and toward Scott. His lover was like a freight train, bearing down with a speed that made Kitt blink. Scott swooped in to grab Kitt by his waist and launched him in the direction of the house. "Go! Lock the door. Karen has called the police."

Then Scott's attention was on Emilio, who charged him with the knife brandished. The second Scott had taken to focus his attention on Kitt cost him. Emilio slashed at Scott's arm, hitting the mark with a bloom of blood that caused Kitt to shriek. He should be doing as Scott had said, but he couldn't stand the idea of leaving the man he loved to face this monster alone. He needn't have worried, however. Emilio only got that one shot. He was no match for a Navy SEAL. Scott didn't skip a beat. Ignoring the cut to his arm, he landed a roundhouse kick to Emilio's stomach, sending the man to his knees while the knife flew from his grip. Kitt raced to take the weapon out of his reach, grabbing it and taking a few steps backward. The sound of sirens wailed in the distance.

With interlocking fists, Scott punched the back of Emilio's neck. The asshole crumpled face-down in the surf and lay still. He would have drowned in that little bit of water if Scott hadn't dragged him by the back of his shirt to the dry sand. He left him face-down, obviously unconscious, yet breathing — *which is frankly more than the fucker deserves.* Kitt didn't feel the least guilty about that fleeting thought.

He tossed the knife to the side and met Scott halfway, throwing himself into his lover's arms. Or at least he started to before pulling back at the sight of the blood dripping down Scott's elbow. Scott was having none of that reluctance, though. He tugged Kitt in close and sat them both down on the sand. The feel of the man's steady breath was a stark contrast to Kitt's own rapid heartbeat. How was Scott not freaking out? Was it merely his training or something more basic — such as swatting Emilio like a fly out of duty and not having any real concern about Kitt's wellbeing?

That stupid and insecure thought was wiped away in the next second as Scott held him close enough to almost hurt while kissing him on the top of the head. "It's okay, baby. You're safe. Jesus God, you're safe. I wasn't too late."

The strain in his voice told the story. Underneath all that combat skill was a man who was terrified. His litany of reassurances seemed to be as much for his benefit as Kitt's. Kitt almost smiled as he returned the hug. "Of course I'm fine. You came just in time to rescue me."

"You were saving yourself. I could see you fighting him. I said you were strong, and I was right." He paused to press another kiss on Kitt's head. "Holy crap, seeing that knife so near you nearly gave me a heart attack."

That reminder had Kitt freeing himself from the embrace enough to grab Scott's bleeding arm. "You're hurt. We need to get this wound bound."

Scott managed to strip his shirt off sufficiently to wrap it around his wound with a quick movement that somehow allowed him to still keep hold of Kitt. "It's nothing. Just a scratch."

Kitt smacked Scott's chest. "Oh my God, don't say something that stupid! I've had cuts. They hurt like hell."

Scott merely grinned and pulled Kitt onto his lap. At that moment, a couple of police officers came running from the house. One of them came to a halt near them while his partner continued on to Emilio. "Scott? What the hell happened here?"

Scott looked up. "Hey, Frankie. How are they hanging, man?"

God, they obviously were old friends, and for a brief moment, Kitt steeled himself to be tossed from Scott's lap. There hadn't been time for their relationship to go public. And with Scott recently coming to terms with his sexuality, Kitt wasn't sure he was ready to be out and proud with people he knew. Scott squashed his fears as easily as he had Emilio by hugging him even closer.

The cop's gaze took the movement in but his expression didn't change. "Still getting into trouble, I see. I guess we'll need EMTs...for both of you?" He tossed his head in the direction of Emilio, who remained out cold.

"Yeeeah," Scott drawled. "He probably has a concussion, although his real problem is that he's a wannabe murderer asshole." He shrugged. "I just got dinged a little."

The cop rolled his eyes before calling for medical assistance. Then he focused his gaze on Kitt. "Are you hurt?" His expression and tone were kind.

Kitt relaxed under the attention. "No, sir. He was trying to drown me but didn't get very far."

The cop nodded. "Glad to hear that, but I'm going to insist you get checked out anyway. I'm sure Scott would agree." He paused. "You've got your hands full, there, son. Good luck." With that, he went to join his partner.

"He seems nice," Kitt observed, not sure what else to say. His mind continued to reel from what had happened, and he felt as if he might break down and cry.

Scott chuckled. "Yeah, Frankie's a good guy. He used to keep me and my summer friends out of trouble here." Scott acted almost as if they were simply sitting on the beach enjoying the day. Of course, he was a trained special operations warrior. That piddling encounter with Emilio probably didn't rank on his scale of hard days.

There were more sirens getting closer, and knowing that they would soon be overrun with other people, Kitt tried to just relax in Scott's hold and enjoy what time he had left with the man he loved. There was no point in denying that truth to himself. A few short days had been all he needed for him to understand in his heart and his head that Scott was the man he'd always been searching for. He wasn't going to be greedy and assume that Scott felt the same way. It would be enough if they kept in touch — maybe he could visit him out in California. Love could grow on both sides if he were patient.

"Have you ever thought of moving again? I mean, I know you're from the Midwest and chose to come east, but would you consider living somewhere else?"

Scott's sudden questions caused Kitt's breath to hitch. "Like...?" He flicked his gaze at him.

Scott stared out at the ocean. "Southern California's beaches are just as beautiful as this one. Although it might seem counterintuitive, the water is even colder out there." Kitt flashed on the memory of his feet hitting the frigid surf only minutes ago. He shuddered. Scott hugged him more tightly.

"I know it's a big thing to ask," Scott continued. "It's just that I don't have a choice about where I live — not while I remain a SEAL, anyway. Sure, I could ask for a transfer to the east coast base, but I don't want to leave my team and it would still be a far distance from here. And while I don't know anything about hairdressing licenses, I expect you could get one out there, right? I mean, you're really good at it, yeah? Karen would slug me one if she could hear me now. She'd have to find another as good as you."

Kitt didn't know what to say. His mind reeled with what Scott was saying. Was it really possible that he was being offered his heart's desire? It seemed impossible, and for sure, he didn't want Scott to do it out of guilt or some outdated notion that he had to continue to protect Kitt or something.

His silence was taken the wrong way. Scott shook his head. "I know this must make me sound like a crazy Emilio-styled controlling asshole."

"No, it doesn't." That was all Kitt had time to get out before they were overrun by EMTs and more police.

* * * *

"Please, Karen, believe me. There is no reason for you to come up." Kitt rolled his eyes at Scott, who was in the process of shooing what had to be the entire police force of the small town out of the cottage.

"Are you sure? It will take me less than an hour."

"I'm fine. So is Scott." He blew out a breath. "Frankly, sweetie, I need a bit of peace and quiet at this point. No offense."

"None taken. I get it. But you have to promise me you'll let Scott pamper you. This whole thing is going to hit you at some point—emotionally, I mean. Scott will know how to handle it. He's good like that."

"He's good like...everything," he couldn't help saying. "We're fine. Please don't worry, and I'll call you tomorrow."

Hanging up, he sat on the arm of the sofa and watched Scott lock the front door and return to him. He stood with his hands jammed in his front pocket, still shirtless and with a large bandage reminding Kitt how his man had taken a knife to the arm in his defense. Scott acted as if the injury didn't exist.

He also picked up their previous conversation as if two hours hadn't just passed. "So, as I was saying... I have a decent apartment, one bedroom, although not really furnished. I have a mattress and box spring, but no bedframe, a small dresser, although there's plenty of closet space, and a big sofa and an even bigger flat screen." He shrugged. "Typical unmarried guy home, I guess."

Kitt couldn't help smiling at that. "Typical unmarried *Neanderthal* guy home is what I believe you meant."

That got a broad smile out of the man. "It can use some decorating for sure. And I have enough money put aside to buy a house. I just never had a reason to do it...before now."

Unable to remain calm in the face of such a seismic shift in his life, Kitt sprang from his perch and grabbed Scott by the waist. "Are you asking me to move in with you?" It seemed obvious, but old insecurities made him doubt it.

Scott wrapped him in his arms, heedless of his injury. "Baby, I'm asking you to marry me. Which, again, I know sounds insane."

Kitt put his finger to Scott's lips, shutting them. "You want to marry me, even though we've known each other for just over a week?"

Scott nodded, then took Kitt's finger away after kissing it. "I don't have much time because of my leave, and once I go back, the chance of being deployed is a constant one. I want you, Kitt. I *love* you. A few days, a few years, a few thousand years — nothing's going to change how I feel. And I know it's a big assumption that you feel the same way or think you ever could, especially after what you've been through.

"The thing is, I want you as my husband so that you have the legal rights and protections that are afforded a military spouse. I want you to have the benefits and support that goes along with that."

Kitt had to blink away sudden tears as he realized what part of those rights would be. "I'd be the one they'd contact if...something happened to you."

Scott's expression gave the answer. "Yeah. I know it's a lot to ask. Being a Navy SEAL spouse is tough. I'm a selfish dick for asking you to take it on."

This time, Kitt shut him up with a kiss. He pressed his now-wet face against Scott's warm chest once they stopped. "I know it will be hard, but not as much as if I let you go. I love you, Scott."

With a whoop, Scott picked him up with one arm and spun him around. Then he kissed him senseless and dropped onto the couch with Kitt on top of him. "I love you, too, baby. Marry me, please, and let me show you how much."

Kitt opened his mouth to say yes, because how could he not? Except there was one more lingering worry. "Are you sure you're ready to be out in front of your teammates?"

Scott ran his hand lightly down Kitt's cheek. "I'm not ashamed of who we are, Kitt. I want everyone to know how wonderful you are and how lucky I am to have found you. I trust my buddies to accept us, and if they don't…fuck 'em. From now on, only you matter."

What was left of the weight generated by his own shame and sense of worthlessness lifted in that moment. He rested his chin on his fist and gazed into Scott's adoring eyes. "So, you're thinking town hall?"

Scott looked affronted. "No, you deserve a wedding with all the trappings. I was thinking right here on the beach…if that's okay with you."

"At sunset?" The idea of marrying Scott against such a lovely backdrop would also help banish the memories of what had happened that morning.

"Perfect." There was a new look in Scott's eyes, one that matched the hardness against Kitt's fly.

Kitt was feeling similarly, but sex would have to wait. "How can we possibly plan a wedding like that in such a short time? I mean, who could pull that off?"

Scott's eyes widened as the answer hit Kitt. They said it in unison. "Karen."

Epilogue

Scott unbuttoned the top of his dress whites. The evening was a warm one. He really should go inside and change into something more casual, but that would mean taking his eyes off his husband, and he couldn't quite bring himself to do that yet. It had only been an hour or so since they'd exchanged their vows and rings. He twisted the band around his finger, enjoying knowing that Kitt had an identical one, feeling as if the shared sign of their marriage bound them physically. In fact, there were quite a few feet between them, as Kitt talked animatedly with Karen and one of Scott's teammates. It still stunned him that a few had taken the time and spent the money to come out to share this special day with him. They had proven that his faith in them had not been misguided. He knew now that Kitt would have that Navy family to support him.

His husband's beauty took his breath away, with his long hair unbound and his trim figure in a white silk suit. The ceremony had been short, yet neither of them had gotten through it without choking up a little bit.

Scott felt no embarrassment over it. How could any man not get emotional when someone as wonderful as Kitt swore undying love and devotion? When he'd signed the marriage certificate as Kitt Carpenter, it had been an amazing surprise. Scott hadn't expected his husband to take his name, had never thought it would matter to him at all. And yet, knowing that his husband carried his name gave him some primeval sense of pride. It was sappy and macho at the same time and he didn't give a damn.

"Jesus, Scott, tuck your tongue back in your mouth. He's gorgeous and all, but we've got a few hours of partying to do before you get to take him to bed." A big hand clapped him on his shoulder.

He turned with a grin to greet his guest. "Dan, I can't tell you what it means to me that you came." On a whim, he'd phoned J.J.'s brother to let him know. He hadn't expected the man to accept the invitation.

"You know J.J. would have been here for you. I'm his proxy, for what that's worth."

"It's worth more than you can know." He looked out at the ocean. "I hope he would have come himself."

Dan smacked him on the side of the head. "Don't talk stupid."

Scott winced, more out of regret for his words than pain. "Sorry. That's my insecurity speaking. This has been hard for me." He could admit that to someone who was his friend as well as the brother of someone he'd loved.

"I'm sure it is. Kitt's obviously worth it, and you know your teammates don't give a damn." He paused for a few seconds. "I bet they're not even surprised. J.J. knew."

Scott whipped his head around. "Knew *what*?"

Dan gave him a patient expression. "That you loved him more than just a friend. He, uh, even considered being more for you just because he loved you so much." He grimaced. "In the end, he didn't act on it because he could never give you what you wanted long term. Please don't carry around misplaced guilt about his death. J.J. always did what he wanted. You couldn't have talked him into anything. And he would want you to be happy."

Scott smiled. "I am."

Dan clapped him on the shoulder again. "Then that's all I can ask as a way to honor him."

Scott didn't have much time to ponder this revelation about his dead friend and how he'd sold him short by not coming clean about his feelings. Kitt was on him seconds after Dan left, his face full of concern, even as he hugged him.

"Are you okay?"

"Yes, baby." Scott held him close. "Dan was reassuring me that J.J. knew all along about my sexuality and how I felt."

"I'm not surprised. From what you've told me, he was a smart and wonderful guy."

They stood in each other's arms as the tide continued to come in. Scott broke the silence. "How about two kids with an option for a third? And I'd like to name one of them Jordan, if you don't mind. It fits for either a girl or boy, and I want to give something of J.J. to the future, now that he can't."

Kitt threw his head back and laughed. "Oh my God, we've been married for like a minute and you already have me changing diapers."

Scott joined in. "Too soon?" He wrapped him in a bear hug and rocked side-to-side in time to the music blaring from the deck. "I can't help it. You're everything I've ever wanted. It scares me that we might never have met."

"Don't think about that." Kitt was warm against his body, his inherent trust doing more to demonstrate and convince Scott of his love than any words. "We can't look back—neither of us. We have to concentrate on the future, and from where we're standing, all I see is hope and happiness."

"Me, too." And with the waves crashing before them, Scott knew it was true.

Man Candy
Samantha Cayto

Excerpt

The IED must have caused brain damage after all, Brent thought as he watched the twink on stage shake his adorable ass. It was the only explanation as to why he had agreed to join his friend Jack at a strip club. Christ, he had always avoided these places in the past. Who needed to pay to watch beautiful boys take off their clothes when it was available for free, plus a blow job, at any gay nightclub?

"Those of us over thirty," Jack had replied earlier in the evening when Brent had wondered out loud.

He was almost right. Brent knew he was good-looking and kept himself in decent shape, too. He had to if he was going to keep up with the troops he embedded with. It was still easy enough to stroll into a club and get cruised by a few guys. Many of them were pretty young, though, and seemed to be getting younger every year. They had started calling him 'Daddy' and that was just creepy. Guys his age were either chasing the younger boys or were past going to clubs. They were home with their husbands, mowing their lawns and raising their kids. Even if he had wanted that kind of suburban bliss, his job as a war photographer made it impossible. His hectic and dangerous work schedule didn't mesh with permanent and everyday responsibilities.

Which left him here, nursing a watered-down bourbon and trying to push back a budding headache. Since the IED had rung his bell months ago, he'd been getting them a lot. Even when they weren't quite migraines, they still made him miserable. The full-blown migraines were hell. Fortunately those were getting fewer and farther between. He pulled out a couple of ibuprofen then slugged them back with a gulp of his drink and a wince.

Jack frowned. "You okay?" he asked during a lull in the music as the on-stage dancer wiggled his ass through the back curtains.

Brent forced a grin. It was nice to kick back and spend time with an old friend without worrying about bullets and bombs. "I'm fine, Mother."

"But you're not enjoying yourself. Want to leave?"

"I am enjoying myself," he insisted. And he was, sort of. His dick was half hard. How could it not be given the amount of hot, young flesh parading in front of him? It would be nice if the music decibels were lowered a notch, that was all. It was going through his head like a spike. Jesus, when had he turned into a cranky old man?

"Look, let's stay for the next dancer and then we can go to this quiet little pub I know that serves real drinks," his friend offered.

His smile was more genuine this time. "Sounds good. I take it you like this boy coming up."

Jack's face transformed into that of a hungry wolf. "Danny, and yeah, he's something special. If I weren't in an exclusive relationship, I'd scoop this boy up and tie him to my bed."

He laughed, understanding the impulse. He and Jack shared a kinky side, although never together. They were both tops and Doms, and neither of them were inclined to switch. Brent's mirth died on a dime, however, as the curtain opened. He caught sight of a compact, lithe body before it became a blur of movement. The dancer executed a series of Olympic-worthy flips down the runway and finished with a twirl around the pole. He stopped upside down, and his eyes pinned Brent to his seat.

Their gazes remained locked for a few seconds. Brent's breath froze in his lungs. His cock swelled to fullness, pressed against the fly of his jeans. His balls ached with growing need. He curled his fingers tightly around his sweaty glass because he couldn't grab the tantalizing flesh literally dangling in front of him. The cherubic face with spiky light hair lured him in like a siren. When the bow-shaped mouth curved in a teasing, knowing smile, a low moan pushed past Brent's lips. The spell didn't so much break as morph as the boy began to twist around the pole.

Jack shot him a grin. "What wouldn't you give to spank that ass?"

Brent covered his eyes and stifled a groan. "Shit, don't put that image in my head."

"Like it wasn't there already."

Between his fingers, he watched the smooth, naked globes outlined by a blue G-string twirl around and around, and couldn't argue with his friend. His palms itched with the desire to grab, squeeze, and hell yes, spank. He had no trouble imagining the beautiful young body splayed across his lap as he put pink on those pale cheeks. He knew he'd be hard and in his fantasy, so was Danny. The boy would cry and beg, but not for Brent to stop. No, he would be eager for the rough play, especially for a good fucking when the spanking was done.

Brent grabbed his drink and choked on a mouthful of crushed ice. It did nothing to ease his hard-on or his contemplation of Danny. The kid was popular — patrons, including Jack, flocked to the edge of the stage. They stuffed dollar bills in his thong. The kid gave each man a teasing grin of appreciation then sent them on their way. Brent didn't want to be just one of the crowd, so he fished a twenty out of his pocket. Pushing up from the table, he sauntered to the runway. He waited for the others to dissipate before he pressed against the edge. When the boy turned his way, Brent held his gaze as he licked the bill and slapped it against a naked ass cheek.

He walked back to his seat and plopped back down. He watched Danny peel the paper from his ass, kiss it with his pink lips, and slide it into his thong. After a wink aimed straight at Brent, he back-flipped his way behind the curtain. The hoots and clapping of appreciation were deafening. Yeah, Danny had lots of admirers. He would remember Brent, though, and that would have to be enough.

He took his time savoring the last drops of his drink, studiously ignoring how his friend sat grinning at him. "Let's go," he finally said to Jack. As he stood to leave, strong fingers encircled his arm. Turning, he saw a sweaty, smiling face looking up at him. Brent stared, temporarily and uncharacteristically tongue-tied. Danny released him and raised a perfectly sculpted arm to wipe drops of water from his brow.

"You're not leaving so soon, are you?" The boy's voice was deeper than he'd expected.

"Um…" was all Brent could manage. Jack snickered behind him.

"I'm going to take a shower." There was a pause before the imp hit him right in the balls with a "Wanna watch?"

He opened his mouth to refuse, but only a little puff of breath came out. Jack laughed out loud and when Brent turned to glare at him, he saw that his friend had sat back down.

"Go on," he urged with a wave of his hand. "I don't think the boy's going to take no for an answer."

"He's right about that, Daddy," Danny all but cooed.

Brent whirled to glare at the stripper. His cock jumped in satisfaction when the boy's eyes widened in trepidation. Good, the kid was smart enough to realize that he'd played with fire.

"Fine," he bit out. "Just don't call me that. I'm no one's daddy, understand?"

"Yes, sir." The tone of voice, submissive, sent a shock of pleasure straight to his groin.

He stifled another groan and waved the guy on. Danny threw him a cocky grin and walked away. Brent fixed his gaze on Danny sauntering in front of him, visions of smacking his taut globes with the flat of his hands dancing through his mind. He followed the stripper into the back of the club where private rooms allowed for a more intimate show. Danny led him into one containing an armchair and a glassed-in shower. Before he could settle himself in the chair, Danny ran his fingers down his arm and clasped his hand. That simple touch was as arousing as if he'd stroked his cock. Brent shivered with suppressed need. Danny smiled as he gently pushed him down to sit. The little cock-tease knew the effect he was having. Straddling Brent's lap, he ran his palms lightly across his own chest and sighed.

"Dancing makes me so dirty," he said in a breathless voice calibrated to arouse. "Shall I get in the shower?"

With fingers clenching the armrests, Brent flitted his gaze down the body in front of him. Smooth pecs gave way to an almost delicate six pack. No pubic hair was visible above the skimpy thong, but a partially hard cock made the silky fabric bulge. Oh, how he wanted to fasten his lips along the ridge. But rules were rules, and he knew that this was not one of those places that crossed the line into true prostitution.

Instead, he growled out a response. "That's what we're here for, isn't it? For you to shower, right?"

The stripper's answering grin was less calculating, proving that he didn't take all this or himself too seriously. "Yeah."

The guy pulled back then, stripping off his G-string and flip-flops, stepped into the shower. The jet head was situated on the wall opposite to where the customer sat, so Brent had a perfect view of Danny's ass while he stood under the spray. When he turned around, Brent could see his rod was now fully erect. Slender and uncut, and God, that bit of information was so fucking hot! Brent imagined sucking it inside his mouth and taking it down his throat. He let the long, low moan of need seep out, knowing that the sound of the shower made it inaudible. He watched with growing arousal as the boy soaped up his body, running hands down opposite arms, across pecs and over a flat stomach. Danny gazed out through the glass, focused on Brent's reaction to him rather than paying attention to where he was washing himself. But Brent couldn't keep from following those hands as they stroked the hard-on jutting out from a cropped tuft of light pubic hair.

Brent's breath labored in his chest. He dug his fingers farther into the cheap leather of the chair's arms. His cock strained and begged to be freed. It wanted to join in the fun. Technically and legally he supposed he could pull it out and jerk himself off. Hell, there was a box of tissues and a wastebasket on the floor next to the chair. He didn't do it, though. He might be ensnared by the exquisite temptation of Danny the Stripper Boy, but jerking off while he watched the guy was way too pathetic. No, he'd get himself off later at home as he relived the show in his mind. Still pathetic, perhaps, just not as much. At least that's what he told himself.

Danny yanked his rod in slow, easy strokes with his legs braced apart and his hips jutting toward his audience of one. When Brent glanced up to his face, Danny's eyes were closed with his lower lip caught between a few teeth. He was a study in pure concentrated bliss. His hips bucked his cock into his hand as his rhythm sped up. Brent's hips rose and fell in imitation of the action without conscious thought. His breathing was harsh and he focused all his attention on the fist pointing the cockhead straight at him.

"That's it, baby," he coaxed in a low tone. "Pull that dick. Come for me. Come. For. Me."

As if the boy were truly under his control, milky white cum shot out of his cock, hitting the shower panel. Danny's echoing cry of pleasure vibrated through Brent's dick. He bent over and groaned with need, his own stubbornness and maybe misplaced pride the only thing keeping him from coming in his pants. Head in his hands, he worked to pull himself together, aware of time ticking away. When he finally opened his eyes, he found that Danny had toweled off and dressed.

"Are you okay?" the boy asked with raised eyebrows. He didn't add 'old man' but Brent heard the words nevertheless.

He straightened and stood up, running sweaty palms down his thighs. "Yeah, thanks."

Danny didn't look convinced. He stared pointedly at Brent's crotch, where his cock still made a hard ridge. "Sorry I can't, ah, help you with that. Club rules, and um, personal boundaries don't allow it."

Brent smiled warmly to show that he understood. "It's okay. I know there's a difference between stripping and whoring."

Danny smiled back. "Thanks. Not everyone does."

Reaching into his pocket, Brent said, "I bet." He pulled a couple of hundred dollar bills from his wallet. "Here, I enjoyed the show."

Danny took the money and frowned as he looked down at it. "Um, this is, like, way too much." His speech pattern gave away his youth even more than his looks.

"No, it's not. You were, like, totally worth it," he replied in gentle imitation.

The boy's face lit up in genuine joy. "Thanks." He reached over and planted a quick kiss on Brent's cheeks. A few inches shorter than Brent, he had to go up on his toes to do it.

Before he could pull away, Brent cupped his jaw firmly in one hand. He swiped his thumb across a soft cheek. "Someone needs to lock you up for your own good, boy," he murmured as he stared down into bright blue eyes.

Those eyes widened in surprise, fear, arousal? Hard to tell, but the lithe body shivered in Brent's hand before he let him go. With a shake of his head, Brent walked out of the room.

"You're too damn young and I'm too damn old," he muttered, although who he was trying to convince was beyond his understanding.

Sign up for our newsletter and find out about all our romance book releases, eBook sales and promotions, sneak peeks and FREE romance books!

About the Author

Samantha Cayto is a Boston-area native who practices as a business lawyer by day while writing erotic romance at night—the steamier the better. She likes to push the envelope when it comes to writing about passion and is delighted other women agree that guy-on-guy sex is the hottest ever.

She lives a typical suburban life with her husband, three kids and four dogs. Her children don't understand why they can't read what she writes, but her husband is always willing to lend her a hand—and anything else—when she needs to choreograph a scene.

Samantha loves to hear from readers. You can find her contact information, website details and author profile page at https://www.pride-publishing.com